TO CATCH A ROOK

ALL THE QUEEN'S MEN, BOOK 1

BY CORA FLYNN

Content Notice

This book is intended for mature audiences, recommended for readers 18+ years only as it contains profanities, sexual innuendo, and detailed sexual scenes.

It contains scenes of graphic violence including but not limited to: torture, murder, gun violence, fighting, castration. It includes graphic sexual scenes including and not limited to: male/male content, pegging, female and male domination, and bondage. It contains mentions of past sexual assault, past addictive drug use, human trafficking, and past death due to overdose.

For a full list of content inclusions, please check my website: www.coraflynnauthor.com.

This is a Why Choose/Reverse Harem romance novel, which means the FMC will end up with more than one love interest and will not have to choose between them to find her HEA. The characters are bi-sexual and will eventually enter into an ethical poly relationship.

This novel is written in American English by a Canadian author, and the spelling, terminology, and grammar have been edited accordingly.

This book has been edited multiple times by multiple people, both personally and professionally, but the imperfection of human beings is a beautiful and inevitable thing. If you notice a typo in any form, please choose to contact me so I may fix it immediately at coraflynnauthor@gmail.com with the subject "Typo Found."

Thank you!

xo
Cora Flynn

Acknowledgments

I have never been more grateful for the incredible support of this community.

When starting my author journey in 2023, I could have never dreamed that writing about a group of characters in a fictional small town solving a large mystery and falling in love with each other in the process could lead me to one of the greatest joys I've ever known.

Hillary's story is very close to my heart. It deals with some heavy subject matter and we get inside the heads of four very different characters as they navigate the complicated paths of their lives.

Life happens to us and life happens for us. We often have to play the game with the hand we are dealt, but with each hand comes a choice, until the bitter or brighter end.

I'm the luckiest person on the planet to have the following people by my side for my own choices and paths forward:

Megan—you are my lifeline and the other half of my soul. Thank you for being a crucial part of this journey. Your creative genius has made this series as marketable as it is. Thank you for believing in me - I wouldn't want to do this without you.

Jennifer—your guidance and wisdom made this story so much better. I'm so grateful to call you a friend, travel buddy, accountabuddy, and sounding board.

Brandi, Paula, Shelby—my Alpha team; thank you for your feedback, good humor, enthusiasm, and love. I can't wait to share this next story with you. You're all so important to me.

Vanessa, Becky, Marina, Kristie, and Emmi—my first ever Beta team. I'm so grateful for your time, energy, and love as you took great care with my book baby. You're the best.

My friends, family, and coworkers—half of which do not understand Why Choose whatsoever, yet continue to cheer me on with all the love in their hearts. You mean the world.

My husband, who is my real-life love story. Love is hard, and sometimes we make it harder than it has to be, but even after 15 years, you're still my greatest cheerleader and advocate. Thank you for supporting yet another dream of mine.

Lara, my editor—your insight is incredible. You've made my words shine and you're a pleasure to work with. I will sing your praises from the rooftops, always.

Maria of Artscandare—your cover design once again knocked everything out of the water. Your talent is just wild.

And of course, you—my readers. Thank you for choosing this book from the mountain on your TBR and diving into the made-up worlds of my head. You've made this small-town Canadian's dreams come true.

XO,

Cora

To all boss babes
Who command their boardroom
And their bedroom

But need to be put in their place every once in a while

You're welcome.

...

CHAPTER 1

Hillary

"Another, Ms. Lane?"

Jeremy, the head bartender of Quintessence and certainly the best martini mixer in all of Carlisle, stared back at me, his tawny eyes filled with a mixture of kindness and pity.

"No."

My response was sharper than I'd intended. Twinges of regret pricked my senses, and I reconsidered my tone. It wasn't Jeremy's fault Kellan had stood me up. Again.

My blond, tattooed, on-again, off-again Viking was one of the best lays I'd ever had, but his work schedule made him incredibly unreliable, and I wasn't the 'doting wife' type. A few meet-ups a year, but he still couldn't show up with any regularity.

It was frustrating, but even more frustrating was to admit I'd been looking forward to this date all week. Kellan had crept under my skin like his own tattoo, and I was going to need that lasered off as soon as possible before it embedded any further.

"No, *thank you*, Jeremy."

I forced a smile on my lips that wouldn't meet my blue eyes and placed my credit card on the counter. "Just bill me for the martini, please."

Jeremy waved a delicate hand dismissively, as if I wasn't the wealthiest person who came through the doors.

"Your money is no good here, Miss Lane. You know that. Winter would have my job."

I stifled an eye roll and picked my black AMEX back up from the polished mahogany bar-top. Winter Wallace, my exasperating best friend and part-owner of the club, was constantly ignoring the fact that I could buy all of her clubs and half of the buildings in this city, refusing to let me pay for anything all because I had gifted her a house one time.

Gifts didn't come with required reciprocation. They were *gifts.* Even after six years, my money still wasn't accepted here. Her stubbornness couldn't match mine, however, and I'd found a way around it.

Guess that's another contribution to little Noble's trust fund.

I couldn't contain the satisfied smirk that spread across my features; if her business wouldn't take my money, her son surely would—when he turned twenty-one. That was twenty years away, so I had lots of time to turn martini payments into a small fortune.

I respected my best friend, but I enjoyed winning a little more. And I always won.

"Now, what's that devious little grin about?"

A smooth, masculine tenor with a strong Irish lilt slid over me like a soothing blanket. The warm presence slid onto the bar stool to my left as an intoxicating mix of cedar trees and something sweet overtook my senses.

A witty comeback sat on the tip of my tongue, but I stopped short when the visage of dark auburn hair and twinkling sea-glass eyes stared back at me.

My assessing gaze took in his solid frame; strong shoulders and molded biceps outlined in a tight, brown leather jacket, a tapered waist and thick thighs perfectly stuffed into tight dark jeans, and a simple, silver Celtic cross pendant hung around his neck.

Attractive didn't do him justice, but not in the traditional suit-men that made up my day to day. This man was a diamond in the rough; unpolished perfection.

And bold, if he thought hitting on me was a wise choice.

"Ahhh, the beautiful blonde is checking me out." The mystery man grinned, showcasing perfectly straight teeth set in full, stubble-accented lips. "Jeremy, it's my *lucky* day."

He tipped an imaginary hat to the familiar bartender as a whiskey tumbler slid down the bar into his open palm.

So, a regular, then. Funny how I'd never seen him before. Not that I was here often enough to be classified as a *regular*, but I was on a first-name basis with most of the staff. That wasn't unique to my businesses, though.

"I appreciate fine works of art," I retorted smoothly, pausing to get off my stool. "I'd say you're more of the Picasso variety, though."

His booming laugh resonated deep in my bones. It was infectious; I couldn't stop the twitch of my own lips at his sly smile.

"And Blondie's got jokes. Forgive me for saying so, but you don't look the type."

He took a long pull of his drink and wriggled a single eyebrow at me. I took it for the challenge it was and stood tall against the bar beside him.

It was rare that a man had the balls to talk to me from a cold call. The men I usually encountered were far too confident, thinking the size of their bank account was equivalent to the size of their dick. Or they had no confidence at all—sweaty, fumbling idiots, terrified to talk to me.

This guy already walked the line of indifferent and brazen, and I was intrigued to find I liked it.

Jeremy stopped wiping a crystal decanter with his cloth and raised a disbelieving eyebrow in our direction.

"I don't believe Miss Hillary Lane has ever been called 'Blondie' before." He shook his head with a muted smile as he started on another cocktail order. "I would tread carefully, Lauchlan. She owns this town, and she'll eat you for dinner."

I winked at my favorite Martini Man; Jeremy always knew just what to say.

"No shit?" Lauchlan—how stereotypically Irish—cocked his head as those depthless green eyes languidly swept up my body. He had a mastery of how to ogle a woman—his eyes didn't linger on one part of my body; instead, he roved over each section like *I* was the work of art, and he was trying to uncover my secrets.

Interesting.

"And here, I thought I would get to have a riveting conversation with a beautiful woman." He shrugged amicably, taking a long pull of whiskey before flashing me a wide smile. "My loss."

I swung my legs back up, my curiosity piqued. Very few people in this city didn't know who I was, which could explain the indifference, but I was willing to learn a little more about the mystery man.

A night of banter and sex with a stranger was probably the perfect antidote to Kellan disappointing me. Again.

With Kellan gone and Aaron deep in the trenches of our upcoming merger, the only action I'd been getting lately was from my wand and my egg. I was all for group activities, but I preferred them to be of the human variety.

"Your gain," I corrected. I lifted my chin in challenge, my eyes adopting my 'take no shit' boardroom persona. "Perhaps it is your lucky day. Make me laugh, Lucky, and I'll buy you a drink."

I shot a fierce boardroom stare in Jeremy's direction, too. "And you *will* take my money if I buy this man a drink, Jeremy."

He held my gaze for a brief moment, then silently nodded agreement. He may be afraid of Winter's wrath, but he was more fearful of me in that moment.

I softened my glare and shot the generally kind bartender a quick wink before I shifted my attention back to Lucky, the sexy leprechaun.

"Okay, *Lauchlan*"—I emphasized his name, though I preferred my nickname much better—"how is it you're a regular and I've never seen you before?"

Another dazzling grin lit up his face and his eyes sparkled with mischief. I was dead-spot-on with the leprechaun persona.

"I'm not a regular. At least, not yet." He shifted his body to face me, resting his head on his raised palm with an amused smile. "Jeremy and I met yesterday, didn't we, Jer-Bear?"

Jeremy shot an unamused glare in Lauchlan's direction, but said nothing, his hands busy making my second dirty martini.

Lauchlan shrugged at the lack of response with another booming laugh, his lazy wink sending a current of desire down my spine.

"Nah, love. I just moved over the pond from Dublin. Da passed, so I came to be closer to my mumsy."

"Mumsy?" I cast a dubious eyebrow at the juvenile term. "Are you a twelve-year-old boy, or is that an Irish thing?"

I had visited Ireland a few times to oversee a few takeovers, but I wasn't an expert on the culture or the slang. I definitely didn't love the word 'mumsy' coming out of a grown man's sexy lips. I did *not* have a 'mommy' kink.

"You don't like 'mumsy'?" Another wink and grin. "Too bad. I was plotting how I could take you home with me tonight to meet her."

"You *live* with your mother?" I nearly spat out the sip of the delicious martini. "I don't think we can continue having this conversation."

Instead of being insulted, the Irish charmer snorted into his own glass of whiskey.

"I just got here three days ago. I'm looking for a place now. Can't stay with Mumsy if I want to take a beautiful woman home with me, now, can I?"

Under normal circumstances, I would not give this man a second glance. He was too unassuming, too charismatic. I liked men who were bossy and brash and ruthless. More like me.

But I'd be foolish if I pretended this man wasn't sex incarnate. I'd be a liar if I said I didn't want to hop on his dick right now. And I'd be an idiot if I didn't take advantage of his undivided attention when all I'd have tonight, otherwise, was a date with Mr. Rabbit.

A woman has needs, after all. Still, I wasn't going to make it *easy*. Where was the fun in that?

"Why would you assume a beautiful woman *would* go home with you?" I retorted smoothly, tapping my ruby red nails against the stem of the cocktail glass. "How do you convince the opposite sex to ride the 'Lucky-train'?"

The air was thickening between us, and the faint scent of juniper and cedar tickled my senses as he leaned closer.

"Oh, not just the opposite sex. I enjoy pleasure in all of its forms, Blondie." He winked his thick brown lashes before rolling his neck back in a sensual muscle stretch, exposing his Adam's apple and a strong jawline.

A delicious heat unfurled in my belly as the visual of this naked man taking part in a debauched orgy flashed through my mind.

Dear god, I need to get laid.

Fortunately, my poker face was better than most. Lauchlan couldn't possibly see the effect he was having on me. I cocked a brow and coolly took another sip of my martini, enjoying the smooth sting as it slid down my throat.

"So, you have the habit of disappointing all genders. That sounds like a poor strategy, Lucky."

Lauchlan clutched his heart and turned back to Jeremy, who was pretending to be busy on the other side of the bar, but undoubtedly listening in on our chit-chat.

"Jeremy, I think I'm in love. Are you notarized? Can you marry us now before she comes to her senses?"

The dignified man rolled his pale blue eyes. "Make him sign a prenup first, Miss Lane. I have a feeling he's of the 'starter-husband' variety."

To my surprise, high-pitched giggles erupted from my chest and I clapped my hands over my mouth to keep them contained. I didn't giggle, not unless my best friend and I had drunk too much wine while watching re-runs of our favorite trash TV.

Lucky-the-leprechaun was turning me into a giggling, silly school-girl. How ... refreshing.

It stuck in my throat as my gaze caught on a familiar set of forms making their way toward a rear booth behind the bar. The lightness in my stomach disappeared; a roiling mass of anger and acid settled into the pit of my stomach instead.

Frederick Lawson, my lawyer, and Aaron Rodriguez, my business associate and sometimes friend-with-benefits, were here together, their heads bowed in apparent deep, quiet discussion.

Frederick wasn't supposed to be having any discussions with Aaron without me present. Our merger was too sensitive, with too many eyes watching—everything had to be handled with extremely delicate care. I needed to be a part of every single statement.

My heated anger froze into shards of ice when I glimpsed Aaron's parents, Veronica and Vincente, and their lawyer, Charles Beckwith, walking at a leisurely pace behind them.

"Whoa, whoa, whoa." Lauchlan held up his hands in a surrender motion as I slipped off the stool, my mouth set in a murderous grimace. "We went from smart-mouthed angel to death-demon in a matter of seconds. What happened?"

"If you'll excuse me." I brushed past him, a flirty night of sex no longer my concern or priority. "I have some business to attend to."

I stomped off to the corner booth, my black Louboutins clacking with menace as I stalked my prey.

I knew my schedule like it was imprinted on my soul, and there hadn't been a single 'emergency' text, call, or email to cross my phone about a meeting today. If they'd reached out to Martin, my executive assistant, he would have been in my ear within seconds—the man was extremely tenacious and valued his job. The audacity of the Rodriguez family to call a meeting without me.

If Frederick hadn't been with me since college, I would fire him on the spot. His retainer was probably the biggest in the city, and there had better be a thorough and believable explanation for this betrayal, or he would find himself out of this job and entire roster of clients.

You didn't fuck with Hillary Lane and get the chance to do it to anyone else.

"Excuse me." I interrupted, not pretending I wasn't out to kill. Five heads snapped up from their conversations and stared at me.

Frederick's cheeks bloomed with a sheepish pink. Charles' crooked teeth flashed in a pompous smirk, while Veronica and Vincente maintained their haughty, pretentious air. Aaron had the intelligence to look somewhat apologetic. For a man with few facial expressions, I would take that for what it was. A caught man and his conniving company.

Billionaires walked a silk tightrope between our friends and enemies. In the years I'd known him, Aaron had become a friend, but his family sat firmly in the enemy camp. Family loyalties were hard to walk away from—I had the jagged scars to prove it—and it was silly to think Aaron would have that luxury.

This move, however, was an act of war.

"So sorry of me, I must have forgotten the invitation to this meeting!" I exclaimed, oozing all the cheerful falsetto I could muster, maintaining my deadliest stare in the process. "How convenient that I was here with a friend when you arrived. I couldn't imagine what this would look like otherwise."

I sidled into the booth, next to a very uncomfortable-looking Frederick. "Now, what is it we are all here to meet about?"

I stared expectantly around the table, daring them to speak first. They were now on the chopping block, and they knew it.

I wanted this merger to go through; it would mean hundreds of millions of dollars in shared assets, and push forward a better way of doing business. Aaron's family was the second richest and accomplished in the state next to the Lane fortune. This deal would be in both of our best interests.

But I wasn't a desperate fool. If I walked away, I'd find other opportunities. I didn't need them to continue my business efforts and grow my enterprise. But they needed me—and it was time they were reminded of that potent little detail.

"No one?" I asked innocently when not even Charles leapt to speak up. "Frederick, why don't you start? Why did the Rodriguez family call a meeting again? I seem to have forgotten."

An awkward throat clearing and a shuffling of papers proceeded the thin, reedy little man's reply.

"Well, ah, Miss Lane"—another throat clearing —"Charles and the Rodriguez family seem to have a few— ahem—*issues* with several items in our current agreement, and requested the opportunity to present their concerns in person."

I slowly swung my head around the table to look each person in the eye. "Oh? How odd. I was under the impression that the terms of the contract were agreed to in full and that the Rodriguez *heir* was the person of authority to sign on behalf of VVR & Company."

I turned a stony face to the man himself. Aaron and I had run in the same elite circles since we were children. If I hadn't already been betrothed in a fucked up modern-day version of an arranged marriage with Logan Eccles, who, funnily enough, was now one of my best friend's husbands, Aaron and I might have been the ones slated to get married.

He was a few years older than me at 35; tall, dark, and handsome, his skin was deeply tanned and his chestnut hair, wavy and chin length, was slicked back and tucked behind his ears. Rich brown eyes with long Latin lashes, full pink lips and high cheekbones made him pretty to look at, but his cold and detached demeanor made him truly captivating.

He was a man on a pedestal; untouchable and uninterested—but not for me. His careful control shattered when I tied him up, begging me to unleash every depraved fantasy on his beautiful body.

And he was a patsy and a puppet for his power-hungry parents—a scenario I was also used to. My own father had narrowly avoided prison for his power-hungry, money-grubbing schemes. Veronica and Vincente were no different—they just hadn't gotten caught yet. I'd made it very clear in our contract proceedings I would in no way work with his parents—it was Aaron and his board, or nothing. Apparently, this was their sneaky work-around.

Charles finally grew some testicles to speak. "Miss Lane, as you are aware, Veronica and Vincente, the *original* Rodriguez founders, are stepping down in order for Aaron to take the helm of the company. Aaron has listened to their reservations about the terms of this agreement and they've come to me collectively for counsel. I reached out to Frederick to highlight a few of their concerns."

"Oh?" I repeated, catching my family's oldest employee's eye in question. We would discuss that later—Frederick might be out of a job, after all.

"Let me make this clear for everyone here, so that I do not need to repeat myself." A shark-like sneer spread across my lips as my gaze trailed around the deathly quiet booth.

"The terms are the terms. They were already agreed to, and I do not take reneging on an agreement lightly. You either move forward, or you don't. I am not negotiating with you."

My gaze settled on Aaron's stony face; I matched his stare with my own. "And *you*"—I tilted my head with a condescending smirk—"I can't continue to see a man who still needs his mommy's permission to play. Call me when your balls have dropped."

His cold fury washed over me from across the table, but as usual, he remained mute. I slid out of the supple blue velvet and stood tall in my five-inch heels, straightening my pencil skirt as if this were just a friendly chat.

"Lovely to see you this evening." I smiled sweetly and wiggled my fingers in a wave. "Frederick, meet me in my office at ten tomorrow, or you're fired."

My heels clacked against the lacquered floor once again, but this time, the sound was triumphant. I searched the bar for Lucky for a tasty little celebration fuck, but he was nowhere to be found. I would have to find another way to burn off this exhilaration.

Hello Mr. Rabbit, my old friend.

CHAPTER 2

Hillary

"Frederick."

I pinched the bridge of my nose in barely veiled exasperation as the dignified man sweated a damp patch through his stiff suit onto my chenille seat cushion.

"Ms. Lane." The shrinking man sputtered slightly, but he managed to maintain his composure while he attempted to grovel his way out of his predicament.

Frederick Lawson had been the Lane family lawyer since long before I was born. By his age and the substantial size of his bank account alone, he could be considered a Lane family heirloom.

But he often forgot he wasn't Daddy's legal counsel anymore—he was mine. And I didn't work backroom deals and scheme with renowned mafia kings in the same ways Daddy did.

Well, not to the same degree, anyway.

"Ms. Lane." Frederick cleared his throat and stiffened his spine in his seat, making him appear an inch taller and ten times ballsier. "I apologize for the lack of communication on my part. The Rodriguez family asked for legal counsel with Charles, and Charles requested I be present to appropriately respond with the—" He faltered, likely realizing he was coming close to insulting me.

"It was very last minute, and I didn't see it prudent to waste your time with another round of inane questions. Charles Beckwith is, quite frankly, an imbecile."

He caught my eye and sniffed, employing the dignified air of a man who thought himself to be far less of an imbecile, but they were one and the same at this moment.

Despite his error in judgment, I believed him. Frederick was the biggest stickler for the written word of law I had ever encountered; so much so, he stood by me and defended my legal right to keep my grandmother's inheritance without giving my father one penny of it, despite my having been groomed to be Daddy's bottomless bank account. He even dissolved the archaic arranged marriage Daddy and his friend had orchestrated, so I could move on with my life.

He wasn't a friend—I didn't even like the man, but he was a formidable ally.

I folded my arms across my silk blouse and leaned back against my desk, my delicate stature hovering above him. "Who requested the meeting? Was Aaron involved, or simply invited?"

Frederick shifted his weight nervously in his chair, but his gaze never wavered. "In truth, Ms. Lane, Mr. Rodriguez appeared very uncomfortable about being present. I can't speak to who invited whom. Charles"—he curled his lip in a sneer of distaste—"was my only contact with arranging the meeting. At a *bar*, no less."

I drew in a deep, cleansing breath, and dipped my head in decision. "Okay. I believe you. But Frederick, no meetings, no phone calls, no discussions of any kind with the Rodriguez family without me."

His balding head shined back at me as he nodded, spewing muttered assurances I really had no time for. I strode around to the other side of my desk and took a seat, scanning the pile of paperwork Marty had set out for me this morning.

"Moving on—where are we with the Blackthorn file?"

After two hours of strategizing for my next two business acquisitions, I checked my phone for messages, absently scrolling through Kellan's chain of texts to the one I'd received last night.

Kellan ViKing: Can't make it tonight. Work stuff.

That was it. A reunion after five months of sporadic texts and missed calls, and that was all he could be bothered to write me by way of explanation.

It was why we could never actually be a real ... anything. Kellan was a gorgeous god of raw power and determination, my equal match in most ways, but his tortured soul and dedication to a family that would literally be the death of him was his most unattractive quality.

He couldn't commit to me so, because of that, I wouldn't commit to him. Who he was letting off steam with in his own time was his business, and I awarded myself the same luxury.

My thoughts drifted to the handsome Irishman, and I allowed myself one solitary minute to undress him from head to toe in my mind before I got on with my afternoon of meetings.

There would be plenty of hot men to distract me when I needed to scratch the itch. I had an important commitment tonight, and I had to prepare.

All thoughts of men and their annoying tendencies left my mind as I called down to my driver to take me to my next destination.

Daddy had summoned, and I was in an ass-kicking mood.

"Miss Lane to see you, sir."

"Ms. Lane, Alaric. *Ms.* Do I look like a twelve-year-old girl to you?"

I cocked a defiant eyebrow at my father's insufferable butler, then pushed past him, ignoring his muttered response.

Alaric was the newest of my father's staff. I couldn't stand the man; he was dismissive, belittling, and a blatant chauvinist, despite the fact *my* money was paying for this home and every paid staff member inside of its walls.

Daddy had lost access to his money years ago because of his own poor choices, and all of his assets, including the ownership shares of multiple companies, had transferred to me. With my grandmother's inheritance, I could have purchased them outright, but the tidy little clause in the fine print handing over his empire to me in case of 'unethical behavior' saved me a wealth of money and time.

He should have been in jail, rotting with the other miserable corpses who wore their greed like a badge of honor, but he knew too many powerful men and he got off with house arrest instead.

Which is why I had been summoned to the monstrous lakeside manor today. As I always was when he needed information about something. His paranoia wouldn't allow him to speak on the phone, and this place, like my office, had to be one of the most secure buildings in the state.

I marched into the room my father liked to spend most of his time. Camden Lane looked up from one of the dusty books in his library and dipped his head in greeting. He was slimmer than most men, his wiry frame taut skin over bones, and his blond hair held more strands of silver than gold.

"Hello, Hillary."

The words were formal—stiff even. An apt description of my relationship with the man since he no longer controlled my future or my assets.

For most of my life, I had been my father's marionette mouthpiece until my ex-husband and my best friend handed me the opportunity to walk away. My father had lost everything because of his own actions, but I had hammered the final nail in his coffin.

I should have screwed it shut instead.

"You summoned, Daddy Dearest?" I folded my arms across my chest and maintained a few feet of distance between us.

We didn't adhere to the false niceties of hugging or outward affection. There were no cameras to pander to, no paparazzi to appease. Just a father and daughter who knew where all the bodies were buried, and the only way to walk away from the graveyard would be to become dead ourselves.

My father sighed, as if my lack of affection was an egregious slight. "Take off your armor, Hillary. I have information that is highly valuable."

I tilted my head disbelievingly, knowing any information from him would come at a cost. "And your price for this information is?"

His opportunistic ass didn't miss a beat. "I would like a day of leave. Please arrange it with him as soon as you're able. There are a few things I must ... attend to."

My brows rose at that admission. There wouldn't be much he could 'attend to' even if I chose to abuse my relationship with Kellan to swing the request for him. He'd be watched like a hawk and would have an FBI escort at the very minimum. As usual, Daddy was playing games to exert what minimal power he had left.

I could deny him the privilege and walk away, but his networks were still vast, and for whatever reason, he still had many loyal associates whispering delicate underground information into his ears.

If I were to grant this request, I could have my own man follow him and report his whereabouts. I might get far more interesting information out of the deal—incriminating information. It paid to be a few moves ahead of my father. He was getting far too comfortable as my parasitic house guest.

I unfolded my arms and leaned against the mahogany desk to my right, maintaining my neutral mask.

"No promises. If your information is as good as you say, I'll speak to Kellan on your behalf this week. Whatever his stipulations are, you're going to follow them to the letter of the law, or no deal."

He met my gaze, holding me in an unyielding stare-off for a lengthy minute, then his tired face broke out into a wide smile.

"Excellent!" He beamed, taking a seat on the austere velvet chemise couch in front of me, patting the seat beside him.

I perched on the end as he reached over and grabbed a thick manila envelope of documents. He took out a single sheet and handed it to me.

"It's to do with the Rodriguez merger. If you look in the rest of the file, you'll find some very damning information."

His triumphant grin turned malicious, unveiling the true man lurking beneath the skin. A man who yearned to plunder and pillage for ultimate power, destroying all good things in his wake.

I tore my gaze away from his sickening smile and skimmed the dossier with growing interest. Veronica and Vicente had dirty hearts and even dirtier hands.

Which would only be a good thing for me.

"Teams are in place, Ms. Lane."

The tinny voice crackled through my earphones as I monitored the security screens in front of me.

"Thank you, Joey."

Josephine, my most trusted vehicle driver, was also a key driver of my operation—the closed-door underground operation that kept many of the key players in this town in check.

I wasn't a single vigilante like Bruce Wayne in Batman. Only a man would be foolish enough to risk his entire empire in a plastic suit.

I had teams. Men and women, elite soldiers, who pledged allegiance to me for a fat paycheck and an entitled sense of justice in a city where there was none.

Tonight, we were going to deliver a powerful message to the very justice system that had a penchant for evil.

"Proceed."

My clipped command echoed over the speakers as my strongest Alpha team—two ex-Marines and an ex-CIA operative—barged into the mansion of the Honorable Henry Cowan, Carlisle's most dishonorable judge.

Black blurred figures swept across my screens, and their body cameras captured the quiet home as they moved into the judge's home office—the office where he was currently entertaining two underage girls.

I hated the time between the moment I had the right information until the moment we could actually go in for the kill. There had been times where we weren't fast enough to catch these sick fuckers in the act, and those failures weighed heavily on my heart in their aftermath.

But my information for tonight had been accurate; my hacker had tapped into Cowan's security feeds, so I knew with certainty the sixteen-year-old twins, still mostly dressed, hadn't yet been assaulted.

Unfortunately, I hadn't been able to stop them from snorting the coke put out for them, so my window of opportunity was now.

A shriek filled the speaker, followed by an indignant "what the fuck!" as Anita, Blake, and Sammy moved into the luxurious den of iniquity. Sounds of muffled grunts and scratchy scuffles resounded around my dark room, followed by more shrieks and then, a howl of pain.

I switched back to the hacked security feeds, since the body cameras weren't grabbing the angle I wanted, and watched Judge Cowan become fully incapacitated in Sammy's hold, his tiny hard dick dangling in front of his pants-less body.

The twin brunettes whimpered, shivering from the coke and adrenaline behind Anita and Blake's bulky forms. My soldiers gently ushered the girls out of the room and into the quiet hallway, leading them back to the nondescript vehicle parked discreetly off the property.

It was a primary rule of the missions: Remove the victims from the premises immediately.

Sometimes, they were brought back to their families—to parents desperate for their return and grateful for our interference.

In other cases, the children were hidden from their families—families who bartered their bloodlines for quick cash or hefty favors. My teams took those to a private facility to heal from their trauma and build skills to start a new life away from the people who'd sold their own souls.

And those families ... well, we dealt with them very differently.

Sammy held up a speaker to our sexual predator, as instructed.

"Hello, Cowan." My velvety voice filled the space as the man spewed futile obscenities. "I'm sorry to have interrupted your party."

He knew my voice; of course he did. No one in the higher echelons of Sequoia society was unfamiliar with my feminine tone.

"What the fuck do you think you're doing?"

This was the ultimate downfall of the ego of a man. Even in the most powerless position with their literal pants down, they didn't understand when they were truly bested. They couldn't humble themselves enough to beg for their lives.

Not that I would kill him tonight. That would be too quick a punishment. Blackmail was a far more effective tool for diminishing a man's fragile image. Why kill him when he could lead me to the entire ring?

Once he stopped being useful, *then* he would meet his end. But keeping him alive didn't mean I wouldn't take a trophy to mark the occasion.

"You know what I'm doing, *Your Honor.* Balancing the scales of justice, taking out one sexual predator at a time. I know you love taking law-defying risks. Care to place a wager?"

The sizable man twisted in Sammy's grasp, but he was no match for the muscles upon muscles built by Sammy's intense training sessions. He gasped from exertion before spitting out an aggravated "fuck you."

Still no groveling, no sense of shame or defeat. It just wouldn't do.

"A barter, then." Cowan couldn't see the malicious smile that crossed my lips, but it was a beautifully dark and dangerous grin.

I was careful in my boardroom. Ruthless, but fair. Brutal, but respectful. Here, behind the hidden door of my secure panic room, I could unleash my demons on those who deserved it and bend them to my will.

It was the ultimate feeling of power.

"I won't be taking your life tonight, Your Honor—but make no mistake, that's what you deserve. Who knows when you'll be useful in the future. I'm not one to waste an opportunity."

I checked the body camera feed to confirm other members of my team had made it back to their vehicle and our packages were secured. All the while I ignored the tirade of the terrified man as he called me a cunt and a whore, and all manner of other words meant to cut down a commanding woman.

I was a cunt with purpose. A whore for justice. A bitch for power. And a slut for a good fuck when the need struck. Sticks and stones, you miserable sociopath.

"Unfortunately for you, I require a sacrifice in exchange. Your days as a sexual predator are over. And while I'd like to trust you at your word, you'll understand why it has no meaning to me."

"What the f–"

Sammy wrenched the sniveling man down to the hardwood floor, and pinned him in place in a hold I had yet to master. He took out a sharp blade from his leg holster and held it menacingly over the pudgy rolls of the judge's stomach.

"Wait! No!"

Finally, raw fear replaced the indignance in Henry Cowan's tone, but it didn't matter. He could have begged for his life at the beginning with an appropriate sense of humility; this would have still been the inevitable outcome.

Sammy waited for my signal, but I held off a minute longer, giving the disgusting excuse for a man one solitary moment to hand me a clue.

"The man you really want is Alvarez! Alvarez supplies the girls!"

Bingo. Alejandro Alvarez, the only mafia fucker who could rival Antonio Carlos, was now moving into Sequoia territory. Until now, I'd had nothing to do with Antonio or Alejandro, but I knew a group of men who did. They dallied on delicate tiptoes with the scum of our society, while I worked to scrub the scum off every surface it touched.

I didn't care who the motherfucker was. If Alvarez was supplying unwilling girls and women in *my* state, he was officially on my hit list. Literally.

I pressed the button on the console in front of me to alert our private medical team, then clicked the signal for Sammy to proceed.

The man had long mastered the art of amputation. He sterilized his hands with a tube of medical-grade sanitizer and removed an ice pack from the small sack on his back, slowly and meticulously, all the while keeping Henry Cowan still as stone between his legs.

I admired his raw strength and skill from afar. It was a reminder I needed to up my training sessions later on in the week.

My best soldier made quick work of removing the judge's penis, and placing it delicately on the waiting ice pack. He placed a black absorbent micro-fiber towel beneath the gaping wound to absorb some of the oozing blood on the floor.

Throughout the procedure, Cowan screamed in visceral agony, his wails and howls obliterating any background noise on my feeds. How convenient he had drugged and seduced young girls in a fully sound-proofed room.

"A medical team is on their way, Cowan. Should you choose to cooperate, they will stop the blood loss and reattach your pathetic excuse of a sex organ. But you'll probably never come again. Let's just call this a precious lesson in self-restraint."

Sammy packed up his things and knelt beside our victim's squirming form, holding the speaker closer to his ear.

"You're mine now, *Judge*. I have all the tapes—enough evidence to ruin your career and put you in maximum security for the rest of your life. When I call, you'd better answer."

Sammy left the makeshift torture chamber, and once he was out of the house, I cut the security feeds and turned off the body cam footage. My teams knew what to do, and I trusted them to get it done. They didn't need me anymore tonight.

Tonight's mission had given me a name; the toxic piece of human filth who sold bodies and stole souls. It was time to dole out the punishment for his crimes.

I'm coming for you, Alvarez.

CHAPTER 3

Aaron

My newest acquisition was truly abhorrent.

I gingerly stepped around the litter of broken needles and dried vomit and breathed through my mouth to avoid inhaling the fetid stench of decay.

I would normally send out my people to do their own assessments, sparing me from this depressing exercise in human depravity. I eyed a rubber hose, its faded orange end peeking out from underneath a soiled mattress, and my stomach churned like a turbulent sea.

The life of a Rodriguez heir was not a clean one. I was not spared from the desolate landscape of the dregs of society simply because I was born in a modern castle with golden faucets and crystal chandeliers.

No, Mother had made it very clear from a tender age I was the product of a sordid empire, which would be my *privilege* to rule one day—with titanium fists and a callousness that put the world's most effective dictators to shame.

I accepted my fate long ago. I didn't strive for a world of 'better and brighter'—what could be better than the life I already had? Men did not accumulate power from soft footsteps and light touches. They took it through bold moves and quiet conversations behind fortified doors.

Acquiring this building was one of the many planned bold moves. A quiet conversation that would secure the Rodriguez empire for our less savory revenue streams.

Money was the ultimate source of security; my wealth could purchase several small countries, and the power our family held reached the far corners of the earth. I didn't require anything else in this lifetime; I strove only to acquire more of each.

They were the only mechanisms that could free me from my prison.

Sebastian Rocher, my personal lawyer and most trusted legal counsel, stood a few feet away from me in the dank warehouse, wearing his own grimace of revulsion.

Long abandoned by its original owners, it was now a drug den for the most damaged of society. But it stood on a crucial piece of territory my company would now legally own—territory we needed to continue our operations and grow our legacy within Sequoia's underworld.

I didn't trust others to carry out this work. One phone call could have spared me from this dilapidated den of inequity, but I had needed to see it with my own eyes. A new player was encroaching on our businesses; I planned to cut him off at the knees before he got the dangerous idea of being invincible.

Even I didn't have such assurances.

Alejandro Alvarez would not come trespassing on my turf without deadly consequences.

My gun felt heavy in its holster beneath my suit jacket as I surveyed the length of the open space one last time, satisfied this move on the board was the right one. I needed to separate my businesses from my parents to ensure my own legacy.

I needed a private fortress to house *my* women, *my* fighters, and *my* money. The Rodriguez family was no longer in alignment, and it was time to set a different course.

"We'll get the cleaners out here immediately."

I turned and nodded to the small, gray-haired man wearing a three-piece suit in the middle of August.

"I want this place sterilized by Monday. I want construction to start before Friday, and the finish date no later than November."

He grunted in acknowledgment. I was presenting our teams with an impossible task, but he didn't question it. To argue with a Rodriguez was a dangerous choice.

I walked swiftly out of the concrete dungeon into the dry mountain air and filled my lungs with the scents of hot asphalt and stale urine—a far improvement from the interior space.

Jacques, my bodyguard, stood to attention beside the black Mercedes G-Wagon parked just outside, awaiting my signal to head to our next location.

The stink of desperation lingered on my skin—I would need a hot shower and a good fuck to take away the stench.

"Club 7," I ordered brusquely and climbed into the soft leather rear seat. Jacques closed the door behind me. I needed a hit of endorphins before my next meeting, and I knew just where to get it.

The leather collar tightened around my neck as a masked, sultry voice purred in my ear. Blood pounded through my veins as I sought oxygen with shallow breaths. The fuzz of near-unconsciousness crept into my vision.

I craved the illusion of no control and not commanding everyone and everything for these little snippets in time. Knowing full well there would *never* be a situation I would relinquish the power I held within my fist.

My release in chains was a small treat to myself on the days I cared enough to pretend I wasn't a dominant, emotionless cretin.

The woman tonight wore black vinyl strapping that only covered her nipples. A pleated skirt barely hid her slick cunt as she slid up and down on my cock in slow, controlled movements. A flogger whipped at my chest and the collar tightened further, keeping me at the finely honed edge of pleasure and pain.

I bucked up into her at a frantic pace, chasing the weightlessness of a fantastic fuck. A final slide of her hips against mine and I exploded, ribbons of my cum flooding into her.

She cried out alongside my animalistic groan, and she was so well practiced, I couldn't tell if it was from a real orgasm. It didn't matter. She didn't work for her own pleasure; she worked for mine, and she was very well paid for it.

Club 7 was one of my less-legal businesses, the revenue stream I had overseen for the better part of a decade, and the one pleasure for which I paid dearly to Antonio Carlos. I refused to deal in unwilling pussy—all our employees were of legal age and worked for us out of their own free will, but we catered to men's and women's less orthodox fantasies.

Recently upgraded, every room had its own sex landscape—anything to fulfill a client's most debauched desire; toys, costumes, torture devices, ropes and binding agents—the most recent upgrade had been virtual reality simulators to fuck in whatever way you pleased—with a willing human participant on the other side.

Club 7 was the only one of my brothels I frequented when I needed a release. Only a few women and men were allowed in a room with me, all personally vetted before they were selected.

I didn't know their names; I didn't need them. They knew my preferences and played their parts well. There was nothing outside of our transaction than a mutual fuck and a minuscule dent in my bank account.

The lithe woman climbed off of me, with dribbles of my cum seeping down her thigh when her feet hit the floor. It didn't give me any sense of satisfaction. The only woman who made my cock jump for another round when I saw my seed dripping from her greedy cunt was Hillary Lane.

"You may go," I ordered dismissively once she released the collar from my neck and untied me from the bed. She nodded once, then made her way through the hidden door in the wall to a fully equipped washroom.

I rubbed feeling back into my wrists as I too, made my way into the private client washroom. Marble tiles and copper fixtures gleamed in the soft yellow light as I stepped into the shower to wash the stink of sex from my body.

Thoughts of Hillary's slim frame writhing in pleasure as she impaled herself on my cock invaded my otherwise quiet mind as I prepared for my next meeting—with her.

She was furious with me, and rightly so. Mother had cornered me into the meeting with Charles and Frederick, and I had wanted no part in it, but the family must look united, whatever the cost. A divided family was a weakened family, and we must never show weakness to our enemies. Or our friends.

Hillary was a friend. A complicated friend. A business associate, an industry leader, a woman whose body I knew as well as my own. She was formidable in her intelligence and goddess-like in her beauty—and she harbored her own darkness that called to mine.

But we could never be more than friends—as much as a marriage would be convenient to cement our business interests, the Lane dynasty could never get so close to the Rodriguez empire without knowing our secrets.

Some things were too precious to give up—even to her.

Regardless, her fury also meant she might never enter the bedroom with me again. Hillary's hot head had reduced to a simmer over the years we'd known each other, but a business betrayal wasn't one she'd likely overlook anytime soon. I would have had more optimism if I had killed her puppy instead of taking an unsanctioned meeting without her.

I finished my shower, changed into a new suit I kept here for these kinds of occasions, and directed Jacques to our next destination.

I was a brave man by most accounts, ruthless, but incurring Hillary's wrath was not a battle I looked forward to.

She was an equal opponent and knew what it took to win.

My gaze caught a tuft of shining blonde hair. She bent over a file of documents in the corner booth of our favorite restaurant, La Belle Maison.

Choosing our usual table was a tactic, I knew. She would remind me of our many moments shared in the same space without saying a word, in an attempt to make me compliant for whatever she was proposing. I stifled a smirk and slid into the plush velvet seat. Most men cowered to her power, but I knew her better.

And I didn't cower. To anyone.

"Hello, *Mi Reina*." I eyed her with a neutral mask as she stared stonily back at my chosen name for her. "Perhaps you are not my queen today. To what do I owe this pleasure?"

A server placed a crystal whiskey glass in front of me with my favorite bourbon. I dipped my head in thanks. I turned my gaze back to find frosty blue eyes narrowed and studying me.

"Cut the shit, Aaron." Darkness invaded the ice as she glared through me. "Tell me why you needed a private meeting with my lawyer, and I'll tell you why I'm ending the contract."

Hillary could handle mergers and acquisitions with a controlled and firm hand but, as expected, she would hold nothing back from me today. I squared my shoulders and chose the path of least resistance.

"I didn't call that meeting, as you are aware." I took a sip of the drink in front of me, relishing its soft burn while I was being roasted on the outside. "Mother did. And I'm sure Frederick and Charles are doing their jobs right now to ensure the agreement suits both parties as instructed. What is this really about?"

"Trust, Aaron. It's about trust." Venom laced her tone as she too, took a casual sip of her martini. "I can't trust that you are not a puppet for your parents. I want nothing to do with your parents, as I've made clear from the start. They're vile creatures who have no loyalty for me, and I don't do business without loyalty."

I cocked my head and assessed her fully. She wore a dark burgundy dress today, the fabric clinging to every curve her small frame possessed. Soft waves curled around her shoulders and a single solitary ruby pendant gleamed from the hollow of her throat; I had given it to her as a friendly present when we agreed to merge our companies.

Another subtle power move—ruthless. I stifled my grin.

"Is it loyalty you crave? Or absolute control? I can't seem to tell the difference."

She responded with a light scoff before she sucked the vodka off an olive and snapped it between her teeth.

"If I wanted to control you, Aaron, I'd simply put that collar you love so much around your neck. I don't control my friends."

Friends. She spoke the word without irony, as if friendship could possibly describe what we were. I had attended every family celebration since we were children, despite our four year age difference. I had watched as Logan Eccles shared her first dance at her debutante ball, though later that night, my lips were the first to kiss her pussy, and my hands were the first to make her come.

I let her put a collar on me to satisfy my need for pretense and her need for dominance, but there was nothing *friendly* about the way I fucked her.

Her sharp brows rose as she scrutinized my flat expression. "Do I have your loyalty, Aaron? If not, I am walking away from this deal right now. I don't need you. You can find someone else to fund your whorehouses."

My mask slipped in slight surprise as the flicker of an arrogant smile traced her lips.

"You think I don't know your secrets, A? You think I didn't investigate every atom of your businesses before I agreed to this deal? I know about the 'other' revenue streams too."

She sat back in her seat, the smug smirk no longer in hiding. "And they suit me. I may need them one day. Gray is a color I'm willing to trade in. But I will not contribute to your businesses without your loyalty. *Undying* loyalty."

I reassessed the woman in front of me. Her fierce eyes stared back, unblinking in her specific request. She knew about our secret brothels with certainty. One secret in a vast sea of deceptions, but it could damage enough in the right hands.

Yet, she was still here, still offering to be a *friend*, although that definition was far more blurred with our alliance.

"You have my loyalty, Hillary." I drained the bourbon with a smooth pull and licked its remnants from my lips. "But I will not die for you." I shifted in my seat, leveling my stare.

"*Undying* is not a commitment I am willing for. That's your own burden to bear."

As my answer satisfied her, she nodded and the fire dissolved from her gaze. Had I told her I would give my life for hers, she wouldn't have believed the lie. In our world of predators and prey, Hillary and I would always herald the top position; she wouldn't choose to lay her life on the line for me, either.

"We have a deal, then." She tucked the remainder of her papers into the small champagne briefcase by her side before sliding gracefully out of the booth.

"Sign the paperwork, Aaron. And be a fucking man about it next time."

I smiled as her perfect form strolled away from me; the confidence of a true ruler. As far as battlefields went, this was a simple win, but I had no illusions—Hillary wouldn't be forgiving this slight with a simple declaration of loyalty. I'd have to put her enemy's head on a spike to prove it.

Metaphorically, of course.

CHAPTER 4

Hillary

"So, he just sat there with his tail between his legs? Just stop."

Martin, my assistant of the last five years and one of my dearest friends, was the poised picture of professionalism at the best of times; at the worst of times, he was a petty, vicious gossip, and I loved him for it.

"The Vs have him wrapped around their knuckles, Marty. Aaron is a force to be reckoned with most days, but for them, he's a soft-balled patsy."

The slim brunette man snickered and sipped his coffee despite the midnight hour. We were seated in the comfortable meeting area of my office, reviewing the last of our notes for the weeks ahead; the rest of my team had long gone home for the day. It wasn't unusual for us to work late when new developments in my business arose, but tonight had been a particularly long strategy session.

Weston, Martin's husband, worked late into the evenings as a named partner for Tracey Williams Law—likely why my star employee never seemed to mind it. I paid him handsomely for the flexibility, but I did occasionally feel teeny twinges of guilt that he was tethered to me during most of his waking hours.

"Anyway." I drained the last of my Sauvignon Blanc with one swallow. "They have some serious decisions to make. This isn't a game to me."

Martin nodded and his light gray eyes turned deadly serious. "I know, Laney. Anyone in their right mind wouldn't walk away from a deal with you—not one this good. He'll come around quickly. Even Veronica Rodriguez wouldn't risk ruining this merger."

I hummed absently and ran the pad of my finger around the rim of my crystal wineglass as I considered what would happen if this merger didn't go through. I'd stay obscenely rich; they'd stay obscenely rich … but the real reason I wanted control of the Rodriguez company was one of my deepest secrets. A secret even Marty didn't know.

The security buzzer sounded. I grabbed my phone off the coffee table and flicked to my camera feed, only half-surprised to see Kellan Carlos brooding on my front step.

I flicked on the microphone.

"Go away, Kellan. I don't have the energy for you tonight."

The hulking man turned to face the camera in the top right corner of the small alcove and quirked a thick blond eyebrow at the screen.

"I can disable your system in two minutes, Hill. Let me in, or I'll come in myself."

I pursed my lips to contain the forming grin. The arrogance of this man was one of my favorite traits about him … and the one I liked to entertain the least.

"Challenge accepted, Mountain Man. Do your worst. The police chief and I are buddies."

Kellan's booming laugh echoed through the tinny speaker of my cell. "I wouldn't count on it. You're scary, Killer, but he's more afraid of me."

He pulled out a thin metal device from his pocket and tapped it against his palm. I stared incredulously as my screen immediately faded to a deep gray then fizzled out entirely.

Martin chuckled beside me. "If I leave now, will the roof still be on this building tomorrow?"

"If it's not, he's paying for it," I grumbled. Despite the circumstances, the butterflies of eager anticipation outnumbered the zings of irritation pumping through my bloodstream.

This building had nearly half a million in security upgrades, yet here I was, just waiting for the big oaf himself to break into my fortress as promised.

If Marty wasn't here and I wasn't so dead tired, I might be tempted to play an adult game of hide-and-seek throughout the stone and glass of the modern loft space, but I was fresh out of fun to give. Kellan had stood me up for the last time; I wasn't about to give him an out before a very satisfying grovel.

The Viking gave me his cock and his kisses on a silver platter, but "I'm sorry" wouldn't be on the menu tonight. The expectation of a grovel from Kellan was as satisfying as a Play-Doh dildo.

One minute and forty-seven seconds later, the shadowy figure of a miniature Hulk strolled through my main office doorway. I tracked his smooth movements through the glass walls of my open office space as he sauntered toward us. A dangerous grin spread wide across his angular cheekbones that shot fiery sparks deep into my belly.

When he officially made his presence known in front of my suite, he leaned casually against the doorway and shoved his hands in his pockets as he jutted his chin in challenge.

"You were saying?"

"My cue to leave!" Martin beamed cheerfully as he slid off the cream leather sofa, grabbing the navy suit jacket he'd tossed between us. He turned to the challenging commando still taking up space in my doorway, and clapped a hand on his shoulder. "Good luck, my friend."

I didn't need to see the wink to know it had come and gone—Marty's cheekiness was his trademark attempt to lower the boiling temperature in the room. It was why we worked so well together. I was a notable hothead, and Martin knew just how to defuse me—most of the time.

Kellan, however, shot the mercury out of the thermometer, toxic fumes be damned. He poked and prodded until one of us detonated—a constant game of apocalyptic cat and mouse.

He grunted in a Neanderthal form of acknowledgment as Martin squeezed past him, but his dark blue gaze never shifted from mine.

A burgeoning silence took over the space, filled with all the words we couldn't say out loud. I breathed evenly through it, determined not to be the first to crack.

Instead, I took in his appearance; his crisp sky-blue dress shirt was unbuttoned at the collar, revealing the myriad of rich, colorful tattoos across his neck and chest. Rolled up sleeves exposed the colorful artwork on his forearms; a black leather cuff bracelet encircled one wrist, and a tasteful, moderately expensive watch on the other.

Thick thighs and firm ass crammed into a tight black pair of dress pants, and the leather loafers on his feet looked like they belonged in a fashion magazine, not on the intimidating Viking king.

"A little songbird told me you'd be here tonight."

His deep voice was as gruff as sandpaper and as smooth as fine silk. The man was a walking dichotomy, treading the line of dark and light with every footstep. A twisted, tortured soul.

A tortured soul who was a *coward.*

My victory at not being the first to speak was short-lived at the realization Kellan had spoken to Winter instead of reaching out to me.

I injected steel straight into my spine and stood to my full height, diverting the heat simmering in my core to fuel the fire in my eyes.

"You don't need to spy on me through your sister-in-law," I retorted dryly and folded my arms across my chest. "You could pick up your phone and call me."

He rose slowly off the door, angling his body to face mine as he mimicked my stance. I knew this tactic well—I used it daily. He wasn't going to FBI-psychology *me* by mirroring my movements to appear less threatening.

"I knew you were mad." He shrugged his large shoulders unapologetically. "A good soldier does a little recon before engaging the enemy."

Before I could blink my eyes, he stood directly in front of me, so closely the heat of his body blanketed mine in a soothing caress.

I pushed away that thought. There was nothing *soothing* about this conversation.

I tilted my head to stare into the dark oceans of his gaze that kept pulling me in despite my best reservations. "Is that what I am now, Kellan? Trust me when I say you don't want me as your enemy."

"I don't want you as my enemy." He echoed, reaching up to tuck a lock of my blonde hair behind my ear. "I want you as my ..."

He trailed off, but not in search of the right words. Our gazes were locked, the clouds of emotions within his pupils clearing as one dominant feeling took hold and matched mine—desperate need.

I had to break the spell. As much as I wanted the sweet release only Kellan's dominant nature could give me, I couldn't continue to dance like a doll on his stage. I wasn't a puppet, and he wasn't my master.

I took a step back, but the heady mix of hormones and lust made me forget the beautiful Italian couch directly behind me, and I fell backwards into its comfortable seat— just what my predator wanted.

The large man's grin was wicked when he leaned over me and brushed his nose against the underside of my jaw, inhaling deeply.

"Kellan," I warned, pressing my palms against his stone chest to push him away. He leaned deeper into me, moving one hand to grip the side of my head. Holding me in place, he nuzzled my earlobe with soft kisses.

"You smell so good, Killer." His firm lips moved down to my pulse point as he brought his legs up onto the couch, locking me between his thighs, his considerable bulk hovering over me. His growing erection dug into the soft flesh of my belly and my panties grew damp at the feel of him.

If I pushed him away, he'd back off. He was dominant, but he would never go against my wishes. As much as I wanted to exert my power and kick him out for the continued lack of respect for my time, I needed his sweet release even more.

Sex with Kellan was its own form of therapy, and I would pay for the service tonight. I could negotiate the terms and conditions tomorrow.

I angled my head to give him better access and surrendered my body to his ministrations. Two large palms cupped my breasts, squeezing with just enough pressure to cause zings of pleasure to ripple down my spine.

God, I missed the feel of him. The smell of him. The heady mix of amber and bergamot washed over me like a calming warm shower as his touch melted away the stress of my day. The blond bastard was an infuriating, overbearing bear, but my most consistent comfort.

When he bothered to show up, that is.

I pulled his lips to mine, sinking into the couch just a little further as he held my mouth hostage. I surrendered to his punishing kiss. His hips pulsed painfully against me as we got lost in the taste of each other—the familiar flavor of longing on our tongues.

His hands moved from my breasts to my hips, tracing the lines of my hip bones through the soft fabric of my dress. I bucked upward, desperate to be closer, to feel the hardness of his cock against my pussy.

"Surrender."

It was my word of permission, the word that destroyed my defenses and set me free. *Our* word.

As I became pliant in his hold, he adjusted my position, laying me down on the wide seat. He gripped my thighs possessively and hiked up my dress to expose my soaked black lace panties.

The Viking knelt down in front of me, brushing his nose against the fabric as he inhaled deeply. His groan resonated against my flesh, shooting electric sparks right to my clit and causing another gush of arousal between my legs.

Instead of ripping the covering away from my pussy, he mouthed me through it, stroking his tongue back and forth in taunting caresses against my heating skin.

His top lip teased at my clit, scraping the stubble through the lace, leaving a burning fire in its wake. His bottom lip worked up and down my slick opening, sucking up every drop of want through the ruined gusset.

I twisted my fingers into his thick hair, to hold him in place as he brought me to a dangerously delicious climax. Kellan shook his head against me, scraping his stubble in the most agonizing way as he reached upward to pin my hands against my thighs, rendering me completely at his mercy.

He nipped at my clit, licked my pussy clean and yet, he never removed the one minuscule covering between us. I shook beneath his hold, locking my thighs around his head as I writhed against his chin, until I was just a teeny push away from—

"Aughhhh!" The sweetest release ripped through me, flooding my limbs with the purest shot of euphoria. I melted into the couch. Kellan's blue eyes filled with wicked, satisfied intent.

"That's a good girl," he praised, raising himself from the couch to hover his engorged crotch over my sated head. "Now, let's take my feral little killer out to play."

His large hands slowly unzipped his dress pants. Free, his massive cock sprang forward, barely missing my eye. He smelled like clean man, salt, and musk, and my mouth watered as I stuck my tongue out for a teasing taste.

When he shuddered beneath my touch, spurring me on to swirl my tongue over his thick head and swallow down the drops of pre-cum weeping from his tip.

A resonating vibration pulsed against my cheek, but it wasn't of the pocket sex-toy variety.

"Don't answer that." Delicately, I stroked my fingers up his shaft and peered into the most haunted eyes I had ever seen, challenging him to choose me first.

I groaned with frustration as Kellan drew back and reached into his pocket for the technological mood-killer. The navy in his eyes crackled as he read through the message.

The smog of hazy lust dissipated in mere seconds as he gracefully shifted his weight off of me to stand. Swiftly, he tucked himself back into his trousers.

My blood bubbled to boiling for an entirely different reason. This was the way it always was—the very cause of my anger. For all of his intentions, Kellan was a slave to his cause and a pawn for his family. I was nothing but a convenient distraction—and most times, we couldn't even get to the 'distraction' part.

"What's Daddy saying tonight?" I sneered, pulling down my light pink dress and adjusting my ponytail. I deepened my voice into a sarcastic drawl. "Come to me, Kellan. The Cartel needs you."

He curled his lip in a threatening scowl. Gone were the two lovers who desperately needed one another, replaced by two leaders of empires with legions to command. Although Kellan's allegiances were far murkier than mine.

"We're not speaking about this, Hill."

"Why? Afraid of who's listening? I've spent a fortune on this building, Kellan—no one, other than you, has ever gotten in unannounced, and that was because I *let* you."

I stood to match his stance, glowering up at his fierce expression. "Please don't make the mistake of thinking I'm some damsel over here. I know everything there is to know about the Carlos Cartel, and I'm not afraid of your family bullshit."

"You should be!" The rage that overtook Kellan's normally neutral face surprised me with its vehemence.

We were no strangers to fucked-up family situations. I had helped him with his own troubles several years ago when his brother and nephew needed a safe place to hide. At no point in the six years since had Kellan shown me any fear for my safety.

Something must be up—with Antonio or his twin brothers—and it was eating at him.

I immediately changed tactics. It would be far quicker to coax Kellan to fess up than it would be to get my PI on it—and that involved some very careful questioning when Antonio Carlos was involved.

"What's going on, Kellan?" I softened my voice and trailed a finger down his chest, staring up at him with genuine concern. "Why are you afraid *for* me all of a sudden?"

I could feel him flexing his fists by his sides, and I absently wondered if his phone would survive the vice grip. His determined glare weakened just a smidgen, enough to let me know he would let down his barrier enough to answer the question.

"He's talking about taking a successor." The words were bit out; whether they were too hard to admit, or too hard to admit to *me*, I wasn't sure, but it didn't matter. If Antonio wanted to name a successor, there was no question in my mind it would be Kellan.

"And with Georgio out of the picture, he wants it to be you."

His throat bobbed with a hard swallow, and he dipped his head in a nod.

"Does the FBI know?"

A shake of the head. "No. And if they do, I'll be more compromised than I already am."

My heart twinged at that tiny, but momentous, admission. Kellan should suffer from multiple personality disorder with the life he had been forced to lead. My ire didn't disappear, but shared its space now with some compassion.

"The world isn't black and white, Kel," I murmured gently. "Most of us exist in the gray."

A dark scowl matched the furrowed brows of a troubled man. "The gray is only going to get people killed."

"And?" I shifted my shoulders back and stared into the deep blue pits of his burning eyes. "People die in this business, Kellan. One cockroach burns and another scurries in to take its place. We're puppet masters, but we can't control all the puppets."

I laughed bitterly at the acknowledgment; if only I could control all the variables of this chess game. Money could buy most things, but it couldn't buy absolution. Good people still burned in hell and bad guys still roamed free. It was why we'd chosen these twisted paths with gnarled moral codes.

We were shrouded in guilt and burdened with sorrow; and people would continue to die.

Jagged glass coated his words. "There are some people I'm trying to *keep* alive. If they weren't such stubborn, ungrateful *brats.*"

My caustic laugh could have burned through lead pipe. "I've never needed your protection, Kellan dearest. Go save someone else's life."

Instead of agreeing, or more likely, disagreeing with me, the Viking lookalike shot freshly sharpened daggers in my direction and then turned away to type with unfiltered fury. He stalked toward the doorway without another word.

"Great chat!" I called after his retreating form. "Don't let the door hit you on the way out, you Barbarian!"

I picked up my phone and tapped into my security cameras to watch him fully leave Lane Enterprises premises and stuff his enormous body into the ridiculous FBI-issued sedan.

Just when I caught a glimpse of a man who wanted to be mine—he withdrew into his cave like a wounded animal. I wouldn't see him for weeks, if not months, after tonight's little charade.

I blew out a frustrated breath, releasing every molecule of exasperation from my lungs so I could move on with my evening. Despite the late hour, I had shit to do, and another Kellan tantrum wasn't going to interfere with the progress I'd made.

I called down to Josephine, my driver, and waited for her to come around to the front entrance with the Land Rover. It was the only safe way for me to travel this time of night, and we had some things to discuss.

My gaze trailed over the now empty parking lot feeds. Despite my grueling work schedule to keep me busy, I couldn't suppress the slight pang in my heart. No matter our history, as long as Antonio held his future in his hands, Kellan would always walk away.

Coward.

CHAPTER 5

Hillary

I held the squirming eight-month-old in my arms with what I hoped to be a loving embrace. My snotty-nosed nephew wriggled and drooled on my designer dress as he beamed up at me with soft hazel eyes.

I grinned at the cheeky spawn of my best friend and kissed the tip of his nose as the amused group of fathers watched from the other side of their kitchen island.

"He looks good on you, Hilly-Willy."

Shane—perhaps the most irritating of Winter's husbands, but a good man, nonetheless—scooped him out of my arms and placed little Noble in the highchair at the other end of the kitchen, already prepped with an array of fresh fruit for his snack.

Winter was in the shower. Cam had gone upstairs to let her know I was here, so I expected her down shortly.

I had arrived early, wanting to get the most of my morning with Winter and her family. We didn't see each other nearly as much as I would have wanted, between our demanding schedules and the four-hour distance between Carlisle and Brenton, so our monthly morning date was a sacred ritual for both of us.

Sometimes the five men in her life left us alone to catch up. Other times, they stuck around to catch up themselves. In the six years since Cascade Falls, they'd wormed their way beneath my defenses, and I had a tender spot for all of them.

Mostly. Shane still pushed my buttons whenever he could, and Logan—because of our history—knew just what to say to light a fuse; fitting, since our relationship had developed into close sibling territory after all we had gone through.

Cam, Travis, and Drew were sweet, doting husbands and fathers. Too sweet for my tastes, but they treated my best friend like gold. For that, I was grateful.

"Versace looks good on me, Shane." I moved to make myself a coffee on the beautifully crafted espresso machine I had bought for Winter as a birthday gift. Really, it was a gift to me, so I could guarantee the perfect cup of coffee whenever I visited. "Your son looks good all on his own. I'm *his* accessory."

Logan snorted and held out his empty mug. I screwed my face up, then took the mug out of his hand. Returning to the coffee grinder, I prepared his coffee the way he enjoyed it best. Strong and bitter—just like him.

"Me too, Hill. Please?" Drew asked hopefully from the other side of Logan.

I turned around and surveyed the four men in front of me. Cam hadn't returned, and I'd bet shares in my company that he and Winter were enjoying a shower together while I played barista.

Get it, girl. It was far more action than I was getting these days.

"Alright, gentlemen. Give me your drink orders and I'll make you the best cup of coffee you've ever had. But as my tip, let's talk about Winter. Tell me honestly—how's she holding up? Talk fast—I don't know how many orgasms Cam's promised her."

Travis shifted uncomfortably in his seat, but of all of them, he would be the first to speak up. "The meds are working. She's in a much better place right now."

Winter had been recently diagnosed with prolonged postpartum depression. It had killed me to watch my sassy, fierce friend become a shell of her former self. I had missed all the signs for months—we all had. But now she had six people monitoring her every move.

Shane spoke up as he wiped a gob of smushed mango from the tiled floor. "She's started her Pilates workouts again. She's wearing makeup again too, although we've all told her she doesn't need it."

"No, makeup is good." I handed a fresh triple-shot espresso to Logan and took a colorful hand-potted mug out of the cupboard for Drew. "That means she wants to take care of herself. Great signs."

"I can hear you, you know." Winter strolled into the kitchen with a serene smile plastered to her pretty face, Cam only a step behind. Her auburn hair hung in wet, darkened waves, and her vivid blue eyes brightened when she saw me.

Freshly fucked, indeed.

"If you want to know how I'm doing, Hill, you can just ask me." She stopped at Noble's highchair and kissed the top of his little blond head. "Or you know, reread the many texts I've sent you, telling you how I'm doing."

I handed Drew his drink and grabbed another mug for Winter. "You lie, Sweets. I have backup in case I think you're trying to spare my feelings."

"It would take a Russian nuke to hurt your feelings," she sassed back, and that alone brought me some reassurance. "I'm trying to spare your *worrying*."

"I'm *protective*, not a worrywart." I shrugged as I passed her the fresh coffee and started on Travis's cup. "We'll talk about this later, when I can corner you properly."

I stopped pressing the coffee grounds and spun to face the group, recognizing the opportunity in front of me. "And speaking of protective, care to tell me why Kellan is back in town?"

Cam stared blankly back at me; his piercing blue eyes careful. "I didn't know he was back in town. We don't talk business, Hillary. We're not putting our family at risk, especially with Noble to consider."

Travis nodded in agreement; his normally smiling lips tight in a firm grimace. "We stay away from the 'family business' entirely, Hill. I have no idea what he's up to."

Winter took a cautious sip of her coffee, guilt flashing across her features. "Okay, I knew he was in town, but not for any specific purpose. When he messaged me, I figured you two had another blowup and it wouldn't hurt for him to apologize."

Her eyes filled with a naïve hope as she posed the question, "Did he? Apologize, I mean."

I barked a disbelieving laugh and rolled my eyes before shifting back to the machine to finish the last two orders. "Yes, Winter, the man who is possibly more stubborn than *me*, waltzed up to my office with flowers and diamonds."

"Too bad," Logan drawled, his grin one of wicked intent. "Make-up sex is the best sex." He winked obnoxiously at Winter before turning his dastardly grin on me.

My annoying bastard of an ex-husband knew just what buttons to push.

"Wouldn't know," Drew said cheerfully, leaning in to kiss Winter's temple. "You're the only one who pisses her off enough to get make-up sex."

"We've had make-up sex," Shane piped up, wrapping his arms around Drew from behind, nipping the tip of his pinkening ear. "And it was very, very good, wasn't it, baby?"

"Enough sex talk, please!" I snapped, shoving the sloshing mug into Cam's waiting hands. I pulled Winter from Travis' hold and pushed her in front of me, aggressively nudging her toward the patio door.

"Time's up—I'm stealing her for the rest of the morning."

"Hey! What about my coffee?" Shane protested.

I didn't miss a step. "Stop pissing me off, Quicksilver. I don't make coffee for delinquents."

"You made Logan's coffee." I caught his grumble before I marched my friend out onto the sunny concrete patio facing the beautiful view of the Rocky Mountains.

We spent the rest of our time together giggling, reminiscing, and catching up on the chaos in our lives.

I made a vow to myself I would keep a sharper eye on Winter in the coming months. I couldn't be in her presence every day, but I'd be in her ear, making sure she never forgot how much she means to me.

Lane Loyalty was a pact for life. And few would ever get such a luxury.

Visiting Winter had been the best pick-me-up treat I could ever give myself, but Cam's Southern cooking was a little too much so. My body wasn't used to processing the pounds of butter in each bite. I hoped my morning run would work it through my system and not out of my pores.

The noxious fumes of burning asphalt and car exhaust filled my lungs, as the traffic symphony provided the perfect beat to set my pace. Pavement rose to meet my feet as I ran through the streets of the busy downtown core. My condo building sat at the edge of a large public park, but it wasn't big enough for my usual ten-mile run, and I got bored of the same landscape every day.

I enjoyed the challenge of dodging vehicles and pedestrians in the most trafficked district in the city, and used my daily cardio as its own practice ground of sorts. Bodyguards and personal drivers were a requirement in my line of work, but when all else failed, we only had ourselves to rely on—a lesson I would never need to learn again.

I didn't run to music, preferring to keep my wits sharp. My runs were the exact opposite of meditation; an exercise in heightened awareness to sharpen my predator instincts.

I felt the redheaded man's presence long before I saw him in my periphery.

"'Allo, Blondie."

Lucky, the apparently always happy leprechaun, smoothly fell into step beside me; our combined width on the sidewalk an obnoxious presence for pedestrians to move around. Still, I didn't move to make any more room for him. He was intruding on my run—he could be the one taken out.

I slowed my pace just enough to take him in. Leprechaun was an unfair assessment; other than his Irish heritage and impish grin, Lauchlan was anything but.

He wasn't slim and taut like Aaron, and he didn't have Kellan's bulk either. He was dressed casually in basketball shorts and a loose tank, revealing temptingly honed shoulders and biceps, decorated with colorful Celtic symbols. Sweat ran down his temples in rivulets, darkening his hair and highlighting the freckles along his cheekbones. His green eyes held my stare, their mischievous glint checking me out in the same way.

Whoever this mysterious man was, there was no denying he was hotter than sin, and he knew it.

I turned to face forward, ignoring him for the remainder of my route. He kept pace, not interrupting my flow, but he ended up putting his headphones back in when I didn't keep conversation.

When I was done, I stopped at my usual park bench by the duck pond across from my home. The condo building had been my first major investment after I received my grandmother's inheritance. The true start of Hillary Lane Enterprises without my father's gruesome shadow tainting its shine.

Lauchlan stepped up beside me to stretch his calves against the wooden platform.

"Christ, Blondie. You gave me a good go this morning, didn't you?" He grimaced as he massaged his hamstrings with large, deft hands.

I continued my own stretches while throwing an unimpressed side-eye. "Don't sign up for the race if you can't take the heat."

He laughed and the masculine, raspy sound settled into my insides with a warm glow. I liked that laugh.

"Are you a stalker, Lauchlan? Should I be worried?"

"Me?" He clutched his chest like my accusation wounded him.

I had a feeling it took a lot to wound this man.

"No, Blondie. Nothing to worry about, Mumsy's place is just around the corner, and I'm a magnet to a beautiful woman. Can't resist the attraction. No impulse control."

Hmmm. Who was his mother? Not that I knew everyone in this neck of the woods, not by far, but to afford a place in this area meant she'd have the income to be running in certain social circles. Circles I would have been a part of over the years.

"Now that I know you're here, we'll have to make this a regular date, ay? I love a woman who can kick my arse."

He winked and plopped himself down on the bench in front of me, stretching his arms above his head, and revealing a taut abdomen with a strawberry blond treasure trail of hair below his belly button.

Hotter than sin, indeed.

"I'll bet you do." I flipped my hair over my shoulder and pushed off from the bench, still discreetly assessing this man's intrusion into my life.

I hadn't looked him up yet—I had far more important things in my life to investigate than a randy Irishman, but I'd make the time soon. He was sex-on-a-stick, but sexy men were a dime a dozen in the world of the rich and the richer. I was more intrigued by his playful nature; it was a welcome reprieve for a man to joke with me.

I *was* intimidating; intentionally, most days. But sometimes, a woman just wanted a great laugh and a good fuck. Not necessarily in that order.

Unfortunately, this morning wasn't the morning for it. I had a day full of meetings and then attending an important dinner with the Governor tonight. There was no room in my schedule for a delicious casual release with a sweaty almost-stranger.

"I have to go." I released my ponytail and fluffed out my frizzing hair. Hot hands held me hostage by my biceps.

"Don't go yet, Blondie." His voice deepened an octave, and the request came on a gravelly murmur as the man stepped into my space. "I was hoping to have coffee with you."

The enticing redhead reached his hand up to tuck an errant strand of sweaty hair behind my ear and his piercing gaze stared through me the moment I let him in.

Lauchlan was an attractive package, but his eyes were the true windows to his appeal. Pale, like the muted tone of sea-glass, they were the farthest thing from dull. They twinkled with a captivating promise of misbehavior, yet held a soft restraint; like nothing you could do would phase him *or* deter him.

I was drawn to him instantly. But today was not the day for personal indulgences.

I stepped away from his hold. "Do you have your phone?"

He pulled it out from his pocket and unlocked it, handing it to me with a playful smirk. I typed in a number on the Notes app, and handed it back to him.

"That's Marty's number—my assistant. Send him your contact information and I'll reach out."

"Is this for business or pleasure, Blondie? Should I make it clear that I want a date, not a meeting?"

His eyes danced as he teased me, and I couldn't help the shadow of a smile on my own lips.

"Message received, Lucky." I shot him a saucy wink before turning to the path that led to my building.

"I like my nickname, by the way!" he hollered after me as I retreated onto the tree-lined path.

I laughed to myself and picked up my pace. Time to slay the day.

CHAPTER 6

Kellan

"**D**rop the fucking gun and put your hands behind your head."

My words were commanding; authoritative. The timbre of a well-trained soldier. Or, as my father expected, a general of war.

The gangbanger, in his early twenties at most, didn't stop his finger from releasing the safety. I let out a frustrated sigh before aiming at his trigger hand and firing my bullet, shooting his finger clean off.

I felt nothing as I barreled toward the sobbing man, now collapsed in a heap on the cold asphalt, screaming in pain as he cradled his amputated hand to his chest.

I had warned him, but he hadn't complied. We were victims or victors of our own choices. Tonight, the gang leader would choose to lose his finger, or lose his life. But the choice would be his to make.

"Where are you getting your guns, Malachi?"

The greasy blond man's bloodshot eyes glared back at me through the evident pain, clamping his lips in blatant defiance.

Death it was, then.

I rolled my shoulders back, the muscles tight beneath my navy suit jacket. I'd already put in a day with bureau duties, following up on the latest investigation that had brought me back to Carlisle. Now I was spending my evening working on the *other* set of responsibilities that ruled my life.

I was getting too old for this. Only two years away from forty, but I might as well be seventy-five. I wouldn't live that long.

I pressed my boot onto his knee and bore down on him. The entirety of my 250-pound frame dislocated his knee cap within seconds. The piercing shriek of pure agony filled the abandoned alley, but no one was around to hear him.

No one but me.

"I'm asking again, Malachi. The twins didn't supply your last three shipments, and the family hasn't sanctioned their distribution. Who supplied the guns?"

I held my boot over his other knee, the actual threat hanging in the fetid air of a dry mountain night. Malachi stared at me through vengeful eyes, but still he said nothing.

I had to admire his ability to look death in the face with such outward hatred. His arrogance reminded me of my brother, another raging man who also chose to lose his life than admit defeat.

I could admire the tenacity, but the misplaced skill wouldn't be doing him any favors tonight.

I cocked my trusty Glock—not the FBI issued handgun currently tucked safely in my sedan, but the pistol I had been gifted on my fifteenth birthday—and pressed the butt of the silencer into the bleeding man's temple.

"You broke our agreement, Malachi. Do you know what Antonio does to people foolish enough to cross him? My brothers are sadists, but he—he is the devil himself."

The sniveling, shivering sack of shit was going into shock, his body violently shaking against the cool metal pressed against his skin. The combination of fear and excess adrenaline coursed through his veins as potent as the strongest opiate.

I had been conditioned against this kind of biological response by the time I was twelve. Fear made the most seasoned soldier a liability—and the Carlos Cartel didn't make allowances for liabilities. Even from the little boys they trained to become men.

I pressed the barrel deeper into his sweating skin.

"Your guns killed that ten-year-old boy last week, you sick fuck. Your guns murdered his mother and maimed his brother. Who should I hold responsible for this, Malachi? You? Or your supplier?" I lightly pressured the trigger; it clicked ominously.

Malachi choked on a desperate sob before succumbing to the inevitable.

"Al-al-varez."

Finally.

I took one last look at the sorry fuck who'd been brash enough to cross the family and shot a bullet into his brain. He fell to the pavement in a slump.

A soothing cold slid through my veins like it always did when I took a life. Malachi Levi was not a good man, and the sorry stain of his sad existence wouldn't bring me nightmares tonight.

I took out a silk handkerchief from my trousers and rubbed it over Old Faithful meticulously before dabbing at the splatter of blood that had misted my cheeks and collar.

My fingers flew as I sent a text to the waiting clean-up crew. Before leaving the alleyway for the warmth of my Land Rover, I took one last look at the oozing corpse at my feet.

Gangbangers. Desperate for power, hungry for notoriety, but with shit for brains and tiny-dick syndrome.

Their kind disgusted me, even as I knew from the law's point of view—the law I spent my day upholding, mostly—I was no different. My actions equally killed innocents, and there was no hope for my redemption.

I rolled my shoulders again and made my way to my vehicle, heading back to my temporary apartment to settle in for the night.

I had a debriefing tomorrow and I wouldn't be keeping the Director waiting.

"How have we not heard about these guys until now?"

I scanned the reams of paperwork strewn in front of me as Patricia Stanhope, my legitimate boss, leaned against the back of the couch, her weathered face pensive as she considered my question.

The woman was a powerhouse—a relic of an old age of crime-fighting, with a reptilian skin and a brain that moved far quicker than anyone I knew—other than my father. She had been the one to find me all those years ago—the one who saved me from a soulless life.

It had come at a cost for both of us.

She tucked wiry silver strands of hair behind her ears before answering—her irritated tell, even though her face remained neutral.

"They're a careful lot, but incredibly effective," she mused, picking up one statement from the table to skim its contents.

"We're talking about huge swindles here—hundreds of millions of dollars in assets from less than ten parties. Artwork, single edition vehicles, drained private accounts...dating back six years. It looks like there's a heist of some kind every ten months or so, and the perpetrators disappear into the night. No trace of their existence—false identities used, state-of-the-art technology and disguises— it's the most sophisticated operation I've ever seen."

Knowing her history with the organization, that was saying a lot. Patricia had built a reputation for being a shrewd shark. 'Trish the Fish' could smell something fishy from ten miles away, and sniff out the culprit quicker than most at the bureau. Though anyone who wanted to keep their balls wouldn't dare to utter the unsanctioned nickname to her face.

Anyone except me—but I had somewhat special privileges. That, and the fact that she wouldn't hesitate to clock me over the head if she felt it was called for—a move HR wouldn't let her get away for anyone else.

"Trish," I murmured quietly, my eyes filled with all the things I wouldn't say out loud. "This is going to take some time. I wasn't planning on being here as long as this is going to take. I"—I swallowed tightly with the admission —"being in Carlisle isn't good for me."

Her steely gray eyes softened, but only a fraction. "I need you here, Kellan. You have your entire team at your disposal. Use them. There are a lot of people breathing down my neck, and God forbid another millionaire loses his favorite trinket. I need this taken care of—quickly. The sooner you solve it, the sooner you can escape this town."

She tidied the papers in front of me and handed the pile over before turning to put on her suit jacket—a not-so-subtle indication our meeting was over.

"And you can tell your brothers to fuck off and do their own dirty work for a change."

There were no secrets between us. She had been there since the beginning, so there couldn't have been. Though I certainly tried. As much as I liked and respected the woman —the only mother figure I'd ever had in my life—I was just as much a pawn to her as I was to Antonio. A weapon to be wielded when the time called for it.

I dipped my head in respect before the staunch woman turned on her heel and left me alone with my thoughts in the makeshift satellite office. It was a nondescript corner suite in one of the many modern high-rises in the downtown core, with just three desk setups and a small couch in its center.

I stood from the cramped couch and stretched my legs. My muscles longed for release; a workout, or a satisfying fuck. After my last run-in with Hillary, I doubted that avenue would be open to me anytime soon.

Hillary Lane reminded me of a younger version of Trish. Fierce and tough, with a tender heart under the spiny shield—if you just knew where to look. Occasionally, she dropped her walls and let me see it, if only during the times I had her stripped bare in front of me, awaiting my instructions.

Images of her naked, tempting body flooded my senses. The swell of her breasts, her plush, pink pussy dripping onto my bed sheets...

The first time I took her to bed was the beginning of my downfall. My cock stiffened to steel at the memories; even though I was the only one in the barren space, I discreetly adjusted myself before I put a hole in my pants.

A workout would have to do, then. I grabbed my bag from beside the door, texting my number two—Maverick Rogers—as I went. The more the team could investigate before I had to step in, the better.

Sequoia County might have been home at one time in my life, but now it was nothing but a prison. And wanted men only survived by avoiding their prisons at all costs.

If only I had that luxury.

"Fuuuuuuck."

The low growl echoed through the shower stall as I filled the sexy muscled ass with my cum. I squeezed the gym rat's cockhead with firm strokes and his body pressed into mine as his own release spurted onto the marble tiles with a shudder.

The workout I had escaped to wasn't enough of an outlet. When the hot redhead at the high-end gym I frequented kept running his eyes over me as I pressed three times my body weight, I seized the opportunity for what it was. A fast fuck to release my demons with a man I'd never have to see again.

He turned in my hold, and a lazy smile spread across his full lips. Sticking his hand under the automatic shower gel dispenser, he spread the slick foam over his palms and onto my heavy cock, still semi-stiff from orgasm.

For a brief moment, I let him soap me up, closing my eyes to pretend this stranger meant something to me; that the heat of his body was mine to own, mine to command.

But he was a means to an end, and he'd played his role. I opened my eyes and clamped my hands over his wrists, pushing him away from me in the cramped space.

"Not a cuddler, huh?"

The hot stream of water still spraying from the shower head muffled his chuckle. He turned his toned body into the stream and lathered himself up, like fucking a man twice his size in a public shower was an everyday activity.

Maybe it was.

It wasn't for me. Being in Carlisle was already making me reckless. It hadn't even been a week. A man in my position couldn't afford to be reckless.

I ignored his teasing and shifted my considerable bulk to walk out of the stall and away from this bad decision. A surprisingly powerful grip tugged on my wet hair from behind. I turned to shoot him a warning glare—a glare that could make most men piss themselves. His playful smirk stopped me in my tracks.

"I like a kiss goodbye after a good ride, mate." He bit his lip and winked a green eye as he continued to soap himself up; his complete lack of intimidation causing me to pause.

Intimidation wasn't about fear; it was about power. In every sexual transaction, I always held the power—with anyone but Hillary. Even then, she handed her body over to me to be worked as I saw fit.

This man didn't bat an eye and his gaze roved over my naked form with blatant lust. Tugging on his dick, he brought himself to half-mast as I stood there, momentarily dumbfounded.

I snapped out of my temporary lapse and growled out an "I don't kiss." Then I shoved back the curtain and stalked through the locker room, leaving the anonymous fuck and his stiffening cock behind.

I'd pay off the manager to remove the smug man from the membership so I could come back and work out in peace without my poor decision sticking to me like a foul smell.

One problem solved—on to face the rest of my shit-filled day.

CHAPTER 7

Hillary

"Again!"

My muscles begged for mercy as I resumed my training in Sammy's gym, working through the obstacle course he had laid out for me.

Before I could catch my breath, a black-cloaked figure came into my periphery and launched at my torso. They grabbed the hem of my athletic tank and pulled me to them in an aggressive tug, quickly latching large biceps around my shoulders and incapacitating me in a choke hold from behind.

Rule one in Krav Maga: stop the threat. I slipped out of the choke hold using the technique an old mentor had taught me and twirled around, my face now at the attacker's crotch.

Rule two: aggressively counterattack on the most vulnerable areas as quickly as possible. I head-butted them hard and satisfaction rippled through me as my skull cracked against their pelvic bone, likely busting a testicle or two.

My attacker shrieked in agony and dropped to the floor, but grabbed hold of my ponytail on the way down. At the yank, my roots stung from the force as I was pulled to the mat beside him.

I let my body go limp for a single moment before gathering all of my strength. Propelling forward, I wrenched away from his tight grip despite the agonizing tingle across my scalp.

He shifted his weight, crinkling the mat material, then moved off of it, coming after me again. I reached for anything to use within changing my stance. My hand closed on the tacky surface of a ten-pound barbell. I swung it backward with all of my might, risking only a brief glance to see it successfully smash my intended target—the attacker's ear.

He stumbled and clutched the side of his head. I took the opportunity to run to the other side of the gym, following the next rule: disengage from the situation. Once successfully out of his path, I searched my surroundings, looking outwards to fulfill the last rule: scan for the next threat.

Despite common misconceptions, Krav Maga wasn't about defeating the other attacker, it was about survival. I had taken up the practice when I was twenty years old. Eleven years later, the principles remained the same.

I sank back against the rough cinder block wall to catch my heaving breath as Taylor, Sammy's sparring partner, ripped off his padded mask and grinned. A deep crimson stained his satisfied smile.

"Good work, *Ojitos*! Take a break." Sammy's call hollowly echoed from the opposite end of the building. Taylor nodded in agreement, then pivoted on his heel to grab his water bottle.

My gaze roamed around the gym's stark interior. Cracked black mats were marred from years of absorbing the brutalities of man. Platforms of varying heights and wrought-iron stairwells mimicked the streetscapes of a city. A few grab bars were scattered randomly throughout the network of pathways.

The gym was mostly used by parkour enthusiasts and street fighting rugrats. Over the last decade, I also made it my personal training facility.

I had found Sammy through a mutual acquaintance; a woman who lost her sister in a dangerous domestic violence dispute. Sammy had helped her train, which had helped her to heal, and when I saw how his guidance transformed her into a methodical machine of fury, I knew I needed a Sammy too.

I wouldn't settle for a knock-off version—a counterfeit trainer. I hired the man himself. Then, when I had all the pieces in place to avenge the women of our city, I found another use for his black ops training.

Sammy wasn't just another loyal employee. He was family.

"I like watching you train."

I snapped out of my post-survival trance at the sound of his voice. The gruff and sultry baritone filled me with a pleasant and familiar sense of calm, before inevitably piercing through me in spikes of irritation.

"I'd say I enjoy seeing you, but that's too infrequent to really count."

Kellan quirked a bushy blond brow at me in muted amusement and folded his arms across the broad expanse of his chest. "This again?"

He was dressed in training clothes. A navy athletic t-shirt molded to his immense form, revealing the shaded masterpiece inked along every patch of exposed skin. His hair was pulled back in a high bun, loose tendrils framing his shadowed cheekbones and highlighting his sharp features.

The beautiful man was physically perfect, but emotionally stunted. I refused to waste any energy chasing after him today.

"You missed a great time while you and your penis were off sulking." I shrugged a shoulder and pushed past him. Grabbing my water bottle from the floor, I turned my back to him and took a long swig.

Strong notes of bergamot and amber washed over me just before his powerful form wrapped around me from behind. His body heat radiated into the drying sweat on my skin. Solid forearms crossed my chest and pressed in on me with enough force to keep me molded to his body.

Bristles of his beard brushed over the shell of my ear while he slid one arm slowly down the front of my chest, his fingers languidly moving downward until they gently traced along the band of my leggings.

"My penis can let off steam elsewhere. But no one can match that smart mouth."

As his tongue traced the outline of my earlobe, for one second I allowed myself to enjoy his touch; to enjoy the way only he could take me hostage and pull me apart. I relaxed into him as his lips traveled further down the column of my neck. He nipped at every spot he knew would make me putty in his hands.

He shifted his weight just the barest amount, enough to bite at my shoulder. I seized the opportunity to drop, twist, and headbutt him right into his sizable ball sac.

"Ummmff." Kellan's pained grunt reverberated through my skull, but I wasn't quick enough to roll to the side. Large hands wrapped around my ponytail. However, instead of an angry pull to cause me pain like Taylor, Kellan lifted me firmly upward in an almost gentle motion until I was standing before him.

His stormy face broke into a brilliant grin. "Good girl, Killer. Next time, shift your force diagonally as soon as you make contact."

I wrinkled my brow, confused but pleased by the praise. The mats squeaked beneath my feet as I took a step backwards, placing a healthy amount of distance between the undeniable magnetism that crackled between us.

I didn't want to acknowledge the heat in his stare, or the growing outline of the bulge beneath his shorts. I changed the subject.

"How long have you known Sammy?"

He wouldn't have made it through the door without knowing the man well. This was a private session I paid heavily for. Sammy would have gutted anyone who'd forced their way through the doors during my training time.

Shutters closed over the Viking's deep blue eyes, taking my lead at the shift in conversation.

"Old family friend," he replied smoothly and picked up a ratty towel from the ground beside him, tossing it at me. I stared at the torn material and flung it back at him, reaching instead for my Egyptian cotton pink one.

He smirked at me knowingly, but I ignored him. I liked nice things and I wouldn't apologize for that.

An 'old family friend' meant the Carlos Cartel had once employed *my* trainer.

When I had come to Sammy, I didn't have the same resources or people at my disposal I had now. I had investigated him to the best of my ability and while finding his past checkered with government-sanctioned murders and ties to illegitimate dictatorships, I had discovered no links to Antonio Carlos.

Although, with the ease he chopped off male appendages, I should have assumed he had some experience working for the most renowned criminal organization on this side of the planet.

I had never questioned his loyalty, and this new piece of information didn't change that. It just ... complicated things. I didn't need more ties to Antonio Carlos in my life.

As if on cue, Sammy stepped out of his office and strode toward us.

"*Hermano*!" He slapped a hand on Kellan's shoulder, even though he only came up to the base of the big man's chin. "*Como estás?*"

Kellan's eyes lit up and he greeted Sammy like an old friend; the two continued their conversation in rapid Spanish while I watched warily. Their amiable smiles and relaxed body language suggested a familiarity I wasn't entirely comfortable with. I wasn't ready to reconcile Kellan with the deeper, darker part of my life.

I had mastered Spanish by the time I was nine, so following their swapped friendly barbs and inquiries about family members was easy enough. It wasn't until Kellan mentioned 'Alejandro Alvarez' that my interest piqued, my spine tingling. Only Sammy and I had heard the name from the judge's mouth.

"What do you know about Alvarez?" I interrupted, not missing the significant look the two men shared at my intrusion.

Kellan's relaxed demeanor immediately shifted into one of commanding control.

"What do *you* know about Alvarez?"

He cocked his head in the way arrogant men do when they were used to compliant subordinates carrying out their bidding. His arms folded across his chest once again in a defiant stare-down.

"Not enough," I admitted. "But if he's coming into our territory, I need to know more." I assessed quickly while considering the various scenarios where Kellan could become an ally in my silent war instead of a critical bystander. I didn't want to work with the man—I couldn't see any scenario where either of us would make it out of a partnership alive—but I'd be willing to trade information for favors, if that's what it took.

He leveled a chilly gaze at me. "I'm not helping you carry out your crusade, kitten."

It was as if he'd read my mind. My eyes narrowed in suspicion. "Are you keeping tabs on me, Kellan?"

"No more than you're keeping tabs on me." His tone was flippant, filled with the irritation in his eyes. "You're playing a dangerous game, Hillary. If I thought forcing you to stop would work, I would have done it long ago. I'm glad Sammy can keep an eye on you."

The licking fires of betrayal filled my vision and I turned a furious stare onto my supposed loyal trainer and hired torturer.

"Shall I strip you of your cock too, Sammy? I've been studying your technique. I'm sure I could make it as painful as you do."

Sammy subtly winced and shifted position to shield his pelvis. His stoic expression barely changed, but he held up his rough hands in a surrender gesture.

"Kellan came to me a few years ago, *Ojitos,* for an entirely different reason. You were training that day, and he said he knew you. I have had nothing to do with his, uh"—he paused, an amused smirk danced along his lips,

71

despite my threat—"surveillance. Alvarez has been causing problems in"—he briefly glanced at Kellan, as if asking permission. The man didn't move. Then Sammy met my gaze and his expression turned serious. "*Other* areas."

Kellan grunted, but did not move a muscle from his position next to Sammy. The two men held themselves in relaxed postures despite their assessing stares, clearly awaiting my next move.

Wise. Given that I wanted to take off both of their heads, and thanks to Sammy's training, I had a pretty sound idea of how to do just that.

"Your *stalking* aside." I spat out the word before reining in my anger. "If you have more information on Alvarez, I need to hear about it. Is it Alejandro or his sons?"

"No." The blond barbarian king grew to his full height before me, his stance becoming that of the Columbian Commando, Antonio's brutal soldier and heir. "Not happening, Hill. I can't protect you on all fronts on this one. I've kept Antonio away from the flesh trade as best I can here. That's all I can do."

Fuck this man. We weren't a couple; we weren't even *lovers*. We were occasional fuck buddies. Nothing more. He had no right over my decisions, my whereabouts, or my empire—the legal OR the less-than-legal operations.

I would beg for him to dominate me in the bedroom, but that was where it ended.

I drew in a steady breath before erupting like a volcano. "For the last goddamn time, Kellan, I don't *need* your protection. Either help me find him, or fuck off."

An icy, bitter fury flooded the brooding man's features. He dipped his head to Sammy, turned on his heel, and stalked off toward the front entrance doors.

"Coward!" I shouted after him. The blood in my veins bubbled over to boiling as he retreated. He didn't even spare me a glance. The heavy door slammed back into place and his violent energy dissipated into the stale gym air.

"I will help you find him." Sammy's determined tone interrupted my mounting fury. "We will find him, *Ojitos.*"

He placed a tentative hand against my back in a rare gesture of comfort. I allowed it as my emotions wrestled within my body.

Kellan *would* help me take out Alvarez. No, rephrase. *I* would help *him*. Evidently, the ballsy man was wreaking havoc in other areas of the criminal underworld, if Kellan was hunting him down too.

The game was set, the race was on. I just had to get to Alvarez first.

CHAPTER 8

Lauchlan

America was a funny place. Near impossible to get a decent pint to put a few hairs on your chest, but you could buy a cuppa dirt from every street corner that would give you gorilla pecs after a few sips.

I poured out the white paper cup of filth into a random planter and continued strolling through the busy downtown streets of the new city I called home.

Pretty nondescript as far as cities went. Buildings. Trees. Stressed-out looking people racing to their next stressful thing. I'd never admit it to Ma, but I missed the heritage buildings and centuries-old architecture she used to yammer on about every time she visited Dublin.

Odd for me to be nostalgic, considering I preferred to go after shiny things. America was very shiny.

I'd set my sights on two particularly shiny things. One of them was about to go into the upscale smoothie bar in the building across from her condo this very minute.

I watched the tempting little blondie walk across the street as if she owned it. She wore a tight blue skirt and white blouse like she'd just come from filming my favorite office porn scenario. Difference being, *she* was the boss and I was the whining little secretary offering up my body to be used for her pleasure.

Wouldn't be a bad way to go, really. I wasn't above degrading myself for a good bit of fun.

I waited another minute until she'd walked into Juice Junkies, then crossed the street myself, weaving through a car or two to make sure I timed it just right. I took out my cellphone and dialed my voicemail before walking through the glass door that dinged upon my entrance.

"I'll have to get back to you on that." I spoke into the phone and checked my watch as if I was pressed for time. "That works for me. Okay, slán."

I hung up and looked down at my phone, opening my text messages to start typing.

"Lucky?"

Bingo.

I paused and brought my gaze up to meet hers. Hillary Lane, goddess of my dreams, stared back at me. A smirk played on her hot pink lips, and my dick twitched to attention in my tight trousers.

Play it cool, Lauch.

"Oy, Blondie." I feigned surprise and looked around the empty juice bar—fitting, because who the fuck wanted to drink the blood of carrots?—and allowed a playful grin to smile back. "Don't tell me you're a health nut too?"

Her gaze wandered up my torso; I dressed in my most expensive suit today—perfectly tailored around my broad shoulders and trim waist, in a navy that was definitely my color. I don't do ties, so the top collar was unbuttoned lazily, something I learned was very appealing to the opposite sex. The same sex too, if we were going by my track record.

"You don't strike me as the 'health-nut' type." Those sky-blue eyes stared through me in mocking humor, and I laughed easily.

"You got me." I grinned ruefully and pointed to the 'frozen yogurt' ad that had popped up across the rolling TV screen. "I'm here for that."

That, at least, wasn't a lie. I'd already eaten my bowl of Fruity Pebbles—one of my favorite parts of America so far was the wide selection of sugar cereals—and I'd round it out with some fro-yo. Nothing like a balanced breakfast.

Her eyes widened in surprise, followed by a very 'unladylike' snort. Fuck me, I liked that sound from her lips.

"I'm still concerned you're secretly a twelve-year-old boy underneath all of that muscle," she said, as she turned back to the counter to make her order. "I'll go with a 'Green Grenade,' this morning, Timothy. I'll add some wheatgrass and an extra shot of protein powder."

Timothy, the barely twenty-something smoothie slinger, nodded and stared at Hillary with stars in his eyes as she bent her head to check a notification ding on her phone.

Don't blame ya, mate. She's my fantasy too.

She turned to wave me over to the register. "Put his order on my bill too, please."

"Some men don't like women to buy things for them." I was teasing, but briefly scanned the menu. I didn't care what I was ordering, but I'd get something, anyway. "I, however, have no ego when a beautiful woman wants to buy me breakfast." I shot her a cheeky wink before deciding. "Chocolate with skittles topping, mate."

You'd have to be a boat away to not see the look of disgust on both of their faces. Like eating that was any worse than a Starbucks 'whipped cream, sugar pumps, flavor this' shyte.

Ol' Timmy handed Hillary her swamp-water cocktail and then made my delicious, flavorful snack. I beckoned toward a neon green and orange booth at the back.

"Got time for a seat?"

After a quick check of her watch, she dipped her head and followed as I led us over to the quiet corner. The space was still empty, because the good people of Carlisle valued their tastebuds this time of morning.

She slid across the bench looking decidedly out of place, but she managed to settle into the vinyl cushion like she belonged there. I unbuttoned my suit jacket and tucked myself into the narrow seat opposite, feeling a bit like the Hulk at a children's supper table.

"Bite?" I offered her the clean spoon, holding it between us in challenge. Little Miss Billionaire Boss could join me in a sugar rush, or keep to her disgusting sludge routine.

"A taste for a taste," she replied, those feisty little eyes narrowing in on my lips.

A taste for a taste would be a *very* satisfying trade this morning. Then she placed her cup of slop in front of me.

My smile melted into a grimace. "Always a tit for a tat with you, eh?"

The devilish twitch of her mouth made me want to dive into all kinds of challenges with her, but today was about a tease, a taste in its own right.

So, I'd play the game.

My shoulders slumped as I sighed in dramatic defeat. "Alright, Blondie, I'll give it a go. Me first, right?"

I grabbed the plastic cup out of her hand, drew the straw between my teeth and took a long pull, swallowing quickly to bypass my tastebuds.

I choked on the thick, seedy sludge and shoved a spoonful of fro-yo into my mouth to smother the disgusting taste.

"I thought you were a badass, but now I know you are. That shyte's dreadful, Blondie. I think that deserves two bites, that."

"One bite." The flicker of amusement betrayed her hard stare. "A deal's a deal, Lucky."

She wrinkled her nose in distaste, but opened her mouth to accept the spoonful I held out. I couldn't take my eyes off her lips as I nuzzled the plastic between them; I imagined those lips around my cock, guzzling my cum like she was swallowing the sugary cream.

I hoped she wouldn't look as revolted as she did right now, though.

"I can't believe you're eating that for breakfast." She snatched the smoothie cup off of the tabletop and washed down my generous offering. "I'm not convinced you're an adult, Lucky."

I wiggled my eyebrows as I sucked another delicious spoonful, fully aware she watched my lips with the same interest. "Lass, where it matters, I can assure you I am *very* much a man."

The fire in her eyes was enough to tell me I hit my mark. That was enough for today.

I tapped a button on my watch, triggering an automatic call to come through my cell. I glanced at the fake name coming across the screen and furrowed my brows in concern.

"Gotta take this, love. Thanks for breakfast."

I awkwardly sidled my body out of the booth for ants, waved goodbye with a wink, then took my very 'urgent' call.

Step one and two complete. Hillary Lane would be calling me soon enough. I was sure of it.

"Thanks for meeting with me today, Lauchlan. Your portfolio is quite impressive."

Marco Alvarez, the eldest son of Silicon Valley's most major player and the world's most major git, took stock of me from behind his mega desk, which was likely making up for a tiny cock.

I looked around the Elon-wannabe's office, or what I imagined his office to look like; stark white, all metal furnishings, and a pretentious titanium sculpture of a human form on display in the middle of the room.

It was worth a bloody seven million dollars. That would normally pique my interest, but it was ugly as sin and wasn't the reason for this 'interview.'

His company hadn't been here long. Rumor had it they'd recently shifted their base of operations to Sequoia on grounds of 'tax reduction.' My connections had landed me a conversation with ol' Marky Mark, but I had to sell myself to get into the fold.

Challenge accepted, of course.

"I'm a lucky bugger who got into app development early," I replied smoothly, feigning humility as much as I was pretending to care about cell phone apps. "I had a great team in Dublin, and I'm still managing that branch remotely, but I'm eager to break into the American market."

The arrogant man's booming laugh echoed through the creepy modern tomb. "I'll bet you do; app development is the fastest growing industry in the world, and American technologies will be at the forefront."

His dark eyes watched me like a hawk before he noted the sizable file on his desk. "Your work is impressive and your track record speaks for itself. I want you on the winning team with us."

What a wanker. Instead of saying so, I pasted on my most gracious smile.

"I'm glad to hear that. When would you like me to start?"

"You'll have a team of twenty. We'll assign you to a few of our current priorities, but you'll have time and flexibility to work on your own projects. Occasionally, we will pull your team for emergency requests, or when needing immediate work done for highly *sensitive* clients."

Oy, there it was. Marky had earned a reputation for dodging the line now and then—it was that line I was counting on.

I took in the sight of him; all smiles and charm from a bloke who'd destroyed as many lives as he had millions. The greedy fucker just took and took and took, until all that was left was a shell of a human being, their soul long sucked out of them. Her soul ˗

I buried that thought, swallowed the bile creeping up my throat and opted for a charming smile of my own.

"And you're okay with me maintaining my ties to my Dublin team? I won't be able to commit to full-time hours."

His eyes darkened, but he grinned wide, like we were scheming boys in a frat house. "We believe in results. If you're as good as your work shows, just get the job done. Whether you take ten hours or a hundred, makes no difference to me."

What a trap that was. Companies said that like it was such a wonderful HR offer, but it was just a smoke screen for not paying people for the actual hours they had to work. Rich people had to stay rich, and all.

"Thank you for the opportunity. I think I'll fit in here just fine."

I stood and held out a hand, not responding to the crushing grip in a clear Alpha male pissing match. Marco scrutinized my expression, looking for weakness, no doubt, and then plunked my tender fist. I'd put it in a bucket of ice later.

"Welcome."

He turned his attention to the computer at his desk, effectively dismissing me. I strode past the twisted hunk of metal and hoped that one day, I'd get to kick the bloody thing over.

Gerta, the young receptionist, smiled apprehensively as I passed her desk.

"I'm in, Gertie."

We'd chatted for a half hour while Marco-the-insufferable left me to wait in his lobby, and she was a sweet little thing I was going to keep close to—she was a bank vault of information, and I'd subtly gleaned enough out of her in that half hour that would have taken me weeks of sleuthing to find otherwise, so we were about to become pals. Best pals.

She beamed at me, her cherub cheeks pinkening. "I'm so glad to hear it! I'll see you soon, Mr. O'Donnell."

Right. Mr. O'Donnell. That would take some getting used to.

I walked out of the glass and steel building with a renewed spring in my step. Ice cream for breakfast, and a job before tea.

Just a few more checks, and I'd be at mate.

CHAPTER 9

Hillary

"What do you have for me?"

Blackbird's brilliant blue hair was a stark contrast against the dark room, even with the backlit computer screen. Her cherubic face widened into a devious grin. "This next batch is hella interesting."

Blackbird had been working with me for three years. In the four years I had been working on my little side project, she was the best hacker I'd hired by a mile, so I'd put her on my permanent payroll.

Of course, before handing someone the keys to my most private business dealings, I had done some investigative work of my own. When she came up squeaky clean—well, other than her highly illegal hacking activities—I invited her to work for me exclusively. She was worth her weight in gold—which, honestly, wasn't saying much since she wasn't even five feet tall and a hundred pounds soaking wet.

"Oh?" I cocked an eyebrow at the screen as I sat in front of the bank of monitors in my private den. "Do tell."

"Sending the files over now." She bit her lips in concentration as she sent through a standard packet of information using our secure servers.

"Care to give me a quick synopsis?" I asked. This was her favorite part of our monthly meet up. The private gossip in these files was unparalleled. Since neither of us could share it with anyone else...

She rubbed her hands together with another shark-like smile.

"So, Kellan, as you requested, is in town on an official investigation for the FBI—something about an international fraud organization. His FBI phone records don't show a whole lot, but his private number has been in contact with the twins and Antonio more than usual in the past two months. His GPS also shows that he's been out a lot at night—*late* at night—down in the Crocks."

This report disappointed me, but I was unsurprised. It was hard to keep tabs on a man like Kellan; his security rivaled mine on the best of days. There was nothing particularly new there, other than a continued relationship with his demon brothers, and the unleashing of his own demons on a few petty criminals.

If Antonio was pulling more strings than usual, I'd have to watch Kellan's back. He was careful on his tightrope, but it didn't hurt to have an extra spotter. Even if he was currently at the top of my shit list.

"Aaron recently purchased a massive warehouse at the edge of the Crocks—one that was abandoned years ago. He bought it through a shell corporation that's owned by another shell corporation, which is solely owned by Aaron Rodriguez himself. He left quite a complicated paper trail for this one, so I'm guessing he doesn't want anyone to know about it. Or why."

She cleared her throat and continued.

"One of my sources said there are whispers that Veronica and Vicente are moving into new underground territory, but no word on whose authority—keep your eye on this one. Alvarez is gaining traction through the dark web, and I'm seeing his stuff everywhere."

I let out a long breath through my nose and steepled my fingers in contemplation. That Alvarez was making headway wasn't a shock. It was a terrible oversight on my part that it had taken this long for me to see how quickly he was moving into our territory, no longer a 'devil-from-afar' that was of no consequence.

I hated Antonio and the Carlos Cartel, least of all for the hell his son had put my friends in my hometown through years ago, but he was the devil I knew, the devil I was planning for. Aaron's sex clubs paid enough of a tithe that the truly depraved side of the flesh economy didn't pay well here.

I was foolish enough to think the reprieve could last in a greedy world of the powerless and powerful. Kellan had admitted he had a part in that, and while I loathed he kept me in his sights but couldn't bother to call, I knew with certainty I could trust him.

I wanted to trust Aaron now, like I could when we were children. Granted, trusting him would mean I wasn't using my underground sources to investigate him and just take him at his word, but I was finding it hard to do that.

I'd had to make a choice, many years ago, about who I would stand for. I had risked the wrath of Camden and chose myself. Aaron pretended to be in control of his empire, but he was a pretty mouthpiece for his parents. This merger was meant to get him out from under the Vs influence, and they were clinging to him like vicious little spider monkeys. It was time for his choice.

Regardless, I would need to make tactical moves against Alvarez, and quickly. First, I would need to know which player mattered more—Marco, Daniel, or Diego. We were all pawns in our parents' pockets, and it would shock me if Alejandro didn't have his sons running the day-to-day dirt. Drugs and weapons were someone else's problem—let Kellan take on those battles. I could only give myself to the girls.

It wouldn't take long before the pervasive claws of darkness overtook everything in its path, and I'd sold my soul one too many times to have another power-hungry asshole bulldoze my sanctuary of safety.

Blackbird, completely unaware of my inner turmoil, continued.

"A woman has been visiting your father for a few weeks now—every Sunday evening. He met her online. His profile states that he has agoraphobia. I'll spare you from the details of what they've been up to."

The snort escaped before I could stop it. Trust Camden Lane to pretend to have a debilitating fear of leaving his home to get the sympathy card and his dick wet, rather than owning up to being under house arrest for the rest of his life. You couldn't make this shit up.

"But you want to hear the juiciest part?"

I rolled my eyes to the ceiling. "Yes. Out with it."

"Okay, so Lauchlan O'Donnell." She paused dramatically, which meant it truly was a juicy piece of information. "Lauchlan O'Donnell is an enigma. He has a very legitimate online profile, but it's all fake. Fake phone records, fake birth certificate. The Lauchlan you know doesn't exist.

"But, using facial recognition software, there is an Irish man matching eighty percent of the mystery man's facial features, which suggests a family member. His name is Liam Donovan. The obituary was in the Connacht Tribune last May.

"What's interesting is that Liam was featured in a European expose after his death. Apparently, he was one of the most successful, uncaptured con artists of his time. And he had an unnamed heir—a son in his late-twenties. Sound familiar?"

Huh. So Lucky O'Donnell—definitely not his real name—came from a family of Irish con artists, had just moved to America, and had suddenly taken an interest in me, one of the wealthiest women in the country.

How coincidental.

Was I naturally suspicious of anyone trying to get into my skirt? Undeniably, it wasn't the first time I had put my hacker on a digital recon mission to check out my men of the hour, and it wouldn't be the last—but with my security, training, and my need for a great orgasm, it wasn't something I spent much mental energy on.

Being rich and successful made me a target. For overenthusiastic affection, or vitriol. It just depended on the day and the flavor of the week. This news was surprising, surely, but not shocking.

Lucky intrigued me in a way most men didn't. You could read most people's motivations within the first five minutes of meeting them. For men in my circles, their readings were very predictable: power, wealth, dominance, control. Usually, a combination of the four. Lucky was evidently playing me, but I had read none of those motivations in his words and actions.

What was his end goal?

Anger was probably the appropriate emotion to be feeling, but the fluttering tingle of excitement in my belly overrode any sense of indignance. It had been a while since I'd played a proper game of chance.

If Lucky thought I was his prey, he was sorely mistaken. It was time for the hunter to become the hunted.

I caught the time on my monitor—Marty would be here any minute with our afternoon schedule.

"Great work, Blackbird. I'll send your next batch of tasks at the first of the week."

"Thanks, boss." She smirked her apple cheeks and the blue screen went black.

I stood, smoothed my skirt, and locked up my fortress. With an extra bounce in my step, I walked down the hallway to brew a fresh cortado.

I loved games. And Lucky was about to learn just how much.

CHAPTER 10

Aaron

"Absolutely not."

I couldn't mask the sneer of disgust as I stared through my father to the ornate wooden cabinets behind him; we were locked in a barely civil standoff in the confines of his pretentiously luxurious office. The warmth of rich burgundy curtains and thick oriental rugs could do nothing to temper the ice in my veins.

Father's frown at my outright disagreement betrayed the simmering rage beneath his skin; the wrath that boiled his blood and blistered his soul was never far from the surface. He was a tempestuous, tortured beast, but Mother

—Mother basked in her brutality with a well-tailored cloak of indifference.

They were a dangerous pair and had raised me to be the same. I held one small part of me away from their greedy claws; my heart was still intact, save for the many sins that marked it. Battered, but not broken. But bitter—so very bitter.

The depths they were willing to dig for power was of no surprise; from their Columbian roots to their American dreams, Veronica and Vicente had no qualms crushing their competition and burying whichever bodies got in their way.

I was no different, but this decision crossed a line I wanted no part in. My stomach soured and acid burned through my chest, but I maintained my neutral mask, refusing to give them an ounce of leverage.

"This is not up for discussion," he snapped, body taut with tension as he leveled his lethal stare at me. "This family is moving in a different direction, and you *will* see it through."

Mother left Father's side with the slippery grace of a python; her light brown eyes calculating as she walked toward me. I often compared her to the snake in the children's story *The Jungle Book*; in the years since she had first read me the tale, she had honed her charm and beauty into fortified weapons, capturing the meek and the innocent with soft words and snaring smiles.

She stopped in front of me; manicured, soft hands took my own. Brushing my knuckles, she stared up at me with a manipulative pout. "Aaron. This is not up for debate. Your father and I have decided, and the deal is done. It is now your place to carry out the terms."

"The clubs are *mine*." I savagely bit out the word, the fury of their mutiny creeping outward to sit atop my skin. "You have no authority to change the terms without my consent."

"Ahhhh, but we do," Mother purred and her eyes darkened with malicious intent. "Who pays the tithe, Aaron? Who brokers the agreements? Are we not the real power players in this arrangement? You manage what we've built."

Her thumbs stroked the underside of my palms, the gesture a small reminder of a simpler childhood, before the mantle of this empire had become my destiny. I pulled my hands from her attempted influence and stepped backwards.

In my early twenties, I'd had no interest in the drug trade and chose to manage the brothel network instead. Eventually, I took over the fighting rings and the general gambling. I had taken a puny enterprise and grew it into a flourishing domain of sexual deviancy. Yet, the labyrinth of false legal paperwork was not in my name or my company's. They owned my empire, and now they were attempting to yank my chains to prove they were my master.

They were not.

"And you believe destroying a partnership with a known ally for a new player is the best move? Antonio will retaliate. You're putting *our* most profitable businesses at risk for the hope of something more."

"We don't do business on *hope*." Father spat the word as if such a thing was the biggest form of blasphemy. "This move will open up additional revenue streams and guarantee our family legacy for generations. Far more than your frivolous decision to merge with that *woman*."

Spittle flew out of his mouth in a rare display of his true feelings. His hate for Hillary Lane and all she stood for broke through his controlled façade.

An uneasy twinge wrenched my gut at the thought of these new revenue streams—the Rodriguez underground businesses thrived in sexual deviancy and counterfeit goods, but had drawn the line at weapons and unwilling whores—

which could only mean that Alejandro Alvarez had promised them a share in the profits of one—or both.

My merger with Lane Enterprises had been a calculated move of my own. The seeds had been planted for my family defection years before when I first became the majority shareholder for our largest company.

To the public eye, it was a mutual decision by all parties to increase our stock value and secure our business interests, but my parents had vehemently been in disagreement. They forced Charles to call the meeting behind Hillary's back, anticipating she would pull out of the arrangement all together.

They didn't know *Mi Reina* as I did. Her loyalty didn't break or bend from just any shift of the breeze, but I knew I would have to tread carefully to maintain it from now on.

My father wanted me to back down, to agree with his sentiments. I had no intentions of doing such a thing. I had promised loyalty, and I would give it.

I leveled the heat of his stare with the icy disinterest in my own.

"That woman is a business associate whom I respect. The merger is done and *my* company will move forward with she and I as the leaders of the next generation. Do not insult my intelligence again."

His fists tightened and the vein in his jaw ticked as he ground his teeth shut, but he said nothing in return. I moved on, unwilling to linger on this father-son dance for dominance; not with the unsettling topic of discussion.

"And who will broker this departure? Who has the pleasure of telling Antonio you will pass the sizable tithe to his rival? Have you secured their coffin?"

Mother's eyes darkened as she placed a placating hand on my arm; her sinister smirk revealed the true *tonto* in the room: me.

"It is the duty of the true Rodriguez leader, no?" Her voice was quiet, the sultry pitch strategically hypnotic, but her words were as sharp as her fangs. "*Your* company is moving forward with a new partner. Who better to share the news?"

Their intentions immediately revealed, I cursed myself for not seeing their plan sooner. The King and Queen of the Rodriguez line were making their moves. Because I would not willingly bend the knee, they would force me to the ground. A pawn to carry out their agenda. My life was of no consequence.

The decision further enforced what I had known all along. I was an heir, not a son. A subject, not a leader. Their displeasure at my actions required punishment. Their confidence in the decision to defect from a long-standing relationship meant they were willing to pay the price.

Even if that price was me.

A somber detachment flowed through me as if it had always been there; my realization set me free from the wanting wisps of a genuine family.

"Consider it done. When I return from the dead, know that you will be the first I kill."

Mother cocked her head and her lips turned down at my outburst, a show of disappointment. Father had the audacity to snort, his hubris on full display now that there were no lies between us.

I allowed a small morsel of my darkness through to the surface of my departing smile. Then I turned on my heel and stalked out of the room, my strides strong and even despite the numbness seeping through my heart to my skin.

Antonio would surely kill me. If not delivering the news, through some demonic means after the fact—the man's reputation for vengeance had its own tales of legend.

I would have to rely on my own allies, though the one I had in mind tasted like ash on my tongue.

The enemy of my enemy was my friend. I would have to fight the urge to shoot him myself.

My fists pounded against the fortified glass of the condo building, although the force behind my swings was rapidly losing steam.

It was late, after midnight surely, and the downtown core of Carlisle was deafeningly still, save for the dull thumps of my palm against the metal frame.

"For fuck's sakes, Aaron!"

Mi Reina's voice filtered through the exterior speakers and infiltrated the stormy sea in my head. A jarring buzzing cut through my senses as the door swung open in front of me.

I had messaged her beforehand to tell her I was coming. I frowned and pushed my way through the glass barrier. It felt like moving through liquid lead, trying to remember if I had sent a message. Perhaps I asked Jacques to send the message.

Jacques, my driver, had dropped me off minutes ago to leave me to my own devices, but he hovered around the corner in the G-Wagon should I need him.

Jacques was loyal. Hillary was loyal. Beyond that, I couldn't be certain.

My feet carried me to the gold-embossed elevator; I could feel her eyes on me as I propelled to the 48th floor to her penthouse; the security feeds broadcast my state for her to scrutinize. She had one of the best systems in the country; I would know. My contractor had installed them for her.

After my parents—*should I even call them that anymore?*—had sent me off to face my fate, I drank many generous servings of bourbon in my study before Jacques took me to douse my pain at Club 7. My usual attendee tried to coax me to life, but my body was not willing to escape into the comfort of her cunt. I left with a soft cock and a hardened resolve.

My addled brain had convinced me I needed the touch of a real woman, someone who had tasted my darkness and shared the bitter notes of its flavor. As the doors opened into the foyer of her penthouse, my mind betrayed me with second thoughts.

"What in the *fuck* are you doing here?"

The beautiful woman strode into the entrance to her home with a fierce frown, the blue in her eyes muted by the dim light. A fuchsia silk robe kissed the tops of her shoulders and draped across her upper arms. Open, it revealed the light blue silk of a cami and shorts sleep set.

Her long blonde hair was up in a high ponytail, and her makeup less face was radiant, despite the violence that filled her features.

"*Mi Reina,*" I rasped, moving toward her on staggering legs.

She stepped back, out of the way of my incoming embrace. "Aaron," she repeated, sounding more exasperated than angry, "what are you doing here? It's two o'clock!"

"I didn't call you?" I cocked my head in confusion; surely, I had let her know I was on my way. I stilled two feet from the heat of her body, my limbs begging to reach out and touch her—to caress her exposed skin with my lips and mark her as mine.

"I don't answer calls at two a.m., Aaron. I have people for that." She folded her arms across her small chest and her pixie nose wrinkled in distaste. "You smell like the brothel. Please tell me I am not your sloppy seconds tonight."

My head bobbed violently. I hadn't entered the woman; my cock wouldn't fulfill my desperate wishes of escape, and had brought me to her home instead.

Hillary would always be my first choice, but she had never chosen me. So, I had people to take her place to satisfy my base urges as a man, but I couldn't bring myself to date a woman, to spend my time with someone and pretend I had any interest in sharing what remained of my soul.

My gaze wandered to the softness of her curves, the rippled outline of her nipples beneath the smooth fabric. My cock stirred to life, finding the woman it truly desired right in front of me.

"No." I rolled the word with finality off my tongue as I moved closer into her orbit. "I needed to see you."

She stared up to meet my gaze, the familiar, velvet sky-blue of her eyes now a shadowed navy, but not shadowed enough to hide how she felt for me. How she could feel the pull of me too.

My palm caressed her cheek, tracing the soft outline of her jaw before holding her in place by the chin to bring my lips to hover over hers. I licked at the seam of her pouty mouth I loved to challenge, and tasted the sweetness of mint toothpaste before plundering her heat with flicks of my tongue.

Her lips parted on a gasp as I forced her to give me what I was so desperate for. My hands roamed to her hips. I lifted her up and she wrapped her legs around me, pressing my growing shaft into the apex of her thighs and grinding her clit against it. I shifted our combined weight to brace against the wall and thrust my hips upward with each nip of my teeth against her swelling lips.

Wetness seeped through her shorts and onto the seam of my zipper; I peeled one hand from my grip on her waist to unbutton my pants and free my aching cock from my briefs.

Frantically rubbing the swollen head against the dampened silk fabric, I shuddered at the sensation. The movement gave just enough friction to rocket tingles up my spine.

I relished a collar, the illusion of relinquishing control while I still held every portion of power, but tonight, I wanted to abandon control all together and fuck her like she was mine to own.

I wanted to brutalize her body with pleasure and pull orgasm after orgasm from her body with my cock so hard inside her I ripped her apart with my cum.

Her pitchy gasps and wanton moans spurred me on. The fingers of my other hand trailed along the inside of her thigh until I pushed the impeding fabric out of my way and plunged my desperate cock into the unholy warmth of her cunt.

"Stop."

My groan reverberated through our bodies. I stilled at the forceful tone, seeking explanation.

"I'm not having unprotected sex with you if you're sleeping with your employees, Aaron. And you're drunk. Let me down."

I slapped my palm against the wallpapered surface in frustration. But I did as she asked. My cock jutted out in front of me like a primed weapon as I stepped back.

"I'll wear a condom, then," I said in acquiescence. I hated condoms, but so in need of release in the moment, I would do whatever she desired.

"No."

The word was uttered not as my lover for the evening, but as the commander of a tightly run ship. The heat in her stare dissolved into a tired wariness, and she deftly tucked my cock back into my jeans. Despite the dramatic change in atmosphere, it hadn't deflated in the least.

"*Mi Reina,* I need …" I trailed off, my mind returning to its previously cloudy state, unsure what to say. I needed her beautiful body? Her splintered soul? Her demons to blend with mine, so we may submit to them together?

Hillary released a long sigh and beckoned me through the dark hallway beyond the entry. "Come, you can sleep it off here."

She brought me to a private suite on the other side of her home. Its windows were covered with dark curtains to block the cityscape below. She turned on a delicate crystal lamp and pointed to the armoire across the room.

"An extra set of pajamas are in there. They should fit you." She nodded toward the ensuite bath to our left. "Toothbrushes are underneath the sink."

I reached for her and caught her hand to pull her into my embrace. "I need you in the morning. You are always my first pick, *Mi Reina*."

A sad smile flickered across her lips so quickly it was barely there. "You'll be gone before I wake up. And we both know that's not true."

She pressed up on her tiptoes for the barest of goodnight kisses, before swiftly leaving the room and closing the door softly behind her.

I struggled out of my clothing as the weight of my day and exhaustion of my night finally seeped through my skin and into my bones. With a quick message on my phone, I sent Jacques home, determined to have breakfast with Hillary in the morning before my busy day.

I would demonstrate my loyalty before succumbing to my death.

It was the last thought in my addled mind before I drifted into dreamless sleep. When I awoke hours later to the rising sun beyond the curtains, I quickly pulled on my stale clothing with a wrinkle of distaste, but a renewed sense of purpose guiding my movements.

My footsteps were light across the tiled great room separating the two sides of her penthouse. I strode to the familiar bedroom, pausing only briefly before slipping through the cracked door.

Mi Reina lay splayed on the California King before me, a dainty ornament amongst the myriad of cushions and bedding. Her pink silk eye mask engulfed my favorite part of her face, and large powder blue headphones covered her ears. The muffled sound of static noise broke through the soft releases of breath that escaped from the pouty lips I loved to kiss.

I took her in, the vision of her peacefully asleep a stark contrast to her authoritative, wakeful presence. How I wanted to crawl in beside her and cradle her in my arms, to brush the tendrils of silky hair away from the crest of her cheeks.

It would be cruel of me to give in to my temptation, breaking her out of her few moments of peace. I slipped out of her room and padded toward the elevator back down to the dark realities of what was to come.

I messaged my private driving service on the way down, allowing Jacques a few more hours of sleep of his own.

My heart was laden with sadness as I met her expectations, leaving her to wake up alone. Should I live through my next steps, I vowed to live up to every promise I'd ever uttered.

My tattered soul would be hers on a platter, but she would have to share it with the devil himself.

Cora Flynn

CHAPTER 11

Hillary

"Where to this evening, Ms. Lane?"

Josephine's gray eyes peered back at me expectantly in the reflection of the rearview mirror. Her long, dark hair had been tugged tight into a ponytail today. The band of her scrunchie matched her standard uniform of a white tailored suit and practical black boots.

My driver and bodyguard, Josephine was a svelte machine of taut muscle and unassuming strength, the remnants of her military days still imprinted beneath her skin.

She had been one of Sammy's recommendations, and after an unorthodox interview where we grappled on the mats of his gym for a few rounds before I reviewed her unredacted history, I was sold.

Her quiet confidence and stoic demeanor were perfect qualities for a protector, and though our relationship was strictly professional—maiming criminals aside—I trusted her implicitly.

Few people in my life knew about my extracurricular activities. Winter, my most cherished friend, and Logan, a man I could now call upon like a brother, were left completely in the dark on purpose. Years ago, they'd had their own trauma to work through, and I wouldn't burden them with my own twisted vendetta.

Marty, my assistant and confidante, had earned my trust and respect one thousand times over, but I would never drag him into the darkness of this world. His high-power lawyer husband made it even riskier to share my underground deeds. Marty was likely not to approve, anyway. At his core, he was too good.

Aaron knew I tread the line between black and white, preferring to keep shelter within the layers of gray, but I was sure my path of vengeance was as discreet as my stealth team. His dirty needs were far less hidden than mine.

I had discovered the Rodriguez house of sex clubs' years before, after completing an audit of Daddy's more illicit expenditures. Camden Lane was a particularly high paying client of Club 7.

To say I'd been surprised to learn Aaron ran all seven clubs in the Carlisle city district was an understatement, but learning his family paid a tithe to the Carlos Cartel for weapons and drug running had been a vase over the head. The Carlos family and their activities were a deathly plague that continued to infect every person I touched.

One Carlos man in particular continued to infect me with *his* touch.

Kellan had secured the building where we were headed this evening, but until I had last seen him at Sammy's gym, I hadn't realized how much he knew. Layers of security, dozens of countermeasures, and false paper trails covered my tracks, but Kellan had somehow gotten through them.

The man was ruthless in his delivery and swift with his own justice, sharply observant and stealthily strategic. He wasn't someone to underestimate, and he'd proven time and time again he got what he wanted, whether or not I was willing to part with it.

If only I could harness that energy for my gain. I could use a king on my board.

Beyond the vehicle, I stared through the shadows shifting into smoking silhouettes as steam rose from the grates within the pavement.

"The Palace tonight, Joey. Please take the back entrance."

She nodded and flicked on her signal light to move into the next lane as I mulled over my strategy for tonight's discussion.

I'd been working to rid this town of sexual predators for the better part of two years. When one was swiftly brought to their knees, another popped up in its place; a continuous cycle of deeply disturbing Whack-A-Mole.

I was playing the long game; men like Judge Cowan were now in my pocket through carefully crafted blackmail, with the expectation these powerful people would use their influence to help remove the most disgusting portion of our society. Those who couldn't further my agenda—the men and women who defiled children and youth for their own pleasure—received a quick defilement in return, and a tracker chip under their skin. Then they were sent home to contemplate their futures.

That they were still alive was the extent of my mercy.

A predator couldn't hunt without its weapon, so I took away their weapon. I didn't bargain with the corrupted for the lives of innocents.

Despite the years in the boardroom and leading companies through crisis, this task had become my greatest challenge. I buried the sharp pangs of frustration before they blossomed and shifted my focus to tonight's activities.

Alec Turner was one of the few I hadn't returned to society with his dick-less tail tucked between his legs. His deplorable actions required a different approach, and he was currently being held in a secured facility a few miles outside of Carlisle's city boundary.

I needed answers. Since Judge Cowan's admission, Alvarez was the name I couldn't get off my tongue. My most trusted ears to the ground were on it, but nothing was coming up as a solid gold lead.

Marco Alvarez was the obvious household name in Carlisle. He and his two brothers owned a few different companies in the area and his family riches were just a few billions less than mine. Their squeaky-clean 'Christian family values' image didn't particularly scream 'underground criminal,' but media alone had shown that outward appearances could be crisp covers for the worst in society.

I didn't know the man very well, but I could bet I'd be seeing more of him in the near future. A boorish invitation sat on my countertop for an upcoming gala of the wealthiest movers and shakers in our circles. I was sure the host, Jediah, would have invited him. The elaborate parties were a chore to attend, but useful; I always left with the most valuable commodity: information.

I would get information from Alec tonight.

Josephine pulled onto a hidden gravel road, cutting the taillights as she approached the warehouse a half mile down the overgrown lane. The building looked abandoned from the outside; the dense trees and rocky terrain a proper deterrent for wandering hikers in these parts. Inside, however, was a state-of-the-art facility that rivaled a maximum-security prison.

In Alec's case, it was.

We slowed as we approached an electric fence gateway that immediately retracted, sensing the vehicle's presence. Muted solar lights lit the path and Josephine drove into the single parking space sheltered on the north side of the building.

"Plan?"

I couldn't see Joey in the dark cab of the vehicle, but I could picture her fierce expression as we took on another criminal. If I allowed it, she would happily torture the deviant herself, breaking his fingers one by one with her little bone hammer. I'd seen her do it a few times; it was fascinating to watch a bone crush under the perfect precision of a well-calculated blow.

"Interrogation, and then we'll improvise." I grinned into the blackness of the vehicle, unafraid of the tingle in my blood at the thought of hurting a thoroughly guilty man. The system was broken, in disrepair beyond saving—so I had built a better one. I wouldn't lose sleep over one less rapist in the world.

My haunted dreams suffered far greater losses.

We slipped out of the vehicle on silent feet, redundant in the stillness of the late night, but I took all precautions with this side of my businesses. I had no plans to get caught until the work was done. And the work would *never* be done.

I unlocked the steel door with an eye scan and thumb print while Joey stood guard behind me. I had checked the site cameras before we'd left, and while I was confident Alec didn't have the brains or the brawn to break out, Joey didn't waste a second as the door swung open, moving around me to clear the perimeter before I could walk down the lightless hallway.

The building held five cells, each equipped with a shower head and toilet and a twin-sized bedroll in the corner. Painted white walls with a washable reflective coating, and bright LEDs flooded the space with bright light twenty-four-hours a day. Instead of metal bars, each room had a front facing wall of tempered bullet-proof glass, three layers thick.

An automated food dispenser released a protein bar and bottle of water three times a day, and my guests received a single roll of toilet paper expected to last them a week.

The rooms were soundproof, impact-proof, and designed for easy cleanup. A polished palace for torture.

A massive storage basement lay beneath the main level, containing a simple, windowless two-bedroom apartment hidden behind a wall of storage shelves. Until this point, I'd not had need of it, but I had only gotten this far in my activities through thorough preparation and patience.

Brilliant white light seared my eyes when Joey opened the next door. Into the prison wing.

Our body language shifted in tandem—we were now performers; good-cop, bad-cop interrogators from a bad nineties drama. Except my hatred wasn't acting, and Joey's thirst for violence wasn't part of a script.

I stopped in front of the large glass window of Alec's cell with Joey firmly planted on my right. Alec lay face-down on his bedroll, in an apparent attempt to shield his eyes long enough to fall asleep.

I pressed the blue button adjacent to the food dispenser unit. Shrill screams of a siren blared through the hollow interior of the sound-proofed booth and Alec bolted upright with a muted string of curses.

I killed the siren, then pressed another button. A small glass hatch opened on the wall in front of me.

"Fuck you, you stupid fucking cunt. I was sleeping!" Alec's voice was gruff from lack of use, but the rough tone couldn't cover the timbre of visceral hate.

"Fuck you, back," I returned calmly, used to his raging barks after all this time.

I once gave in to his taunts, releasing the wrath that lived in my veins like an infectious parasite. I pounded my fists into his face and kidneys until he was unconscious. Joey had silently stood guard behind me. Beating him to near death had been cathartic—for a little while—until I realized I would likely slip one day; I would truly snap his spine or burst an organ, and death would release Alec from my torture.

I had sworn he would never get the luxury of leaving this world free from his sins in the nothingness of an afterlife. I then created an environment specifically for him, so that every day he would wish for death, and yet every day, I would not grant it.

I assessed his frail frame and frantic eyes, searching for any signs of his strength returning since my last visit a few months ago. It hadn't. A year of 800 calories a day had not been kind.

When I had first been introduced to Alec Turner, he was handsome; pale, pearly skin with red lips and dark brown eyes, coal-black hair framed his face in tousled curls. He had been tall and lean, and powerful.

Now he was gaunt; greasy hair lay in matted clumps down his back, and his eyes held a half-crazed glaze from his time in captivity.

"I'm here with a few questions for you." I folded my arms and leaned forward so my voice carried better into the small space. "Answer well, and I'll up your food rations. Answer poorly, and I'll take a meal away. Understood?"

He tried to spit at the glass in protest, but the puny dribble of spittle didn't even make it past his chin.

"Fuck you."

When he loped to the side of his cot, I noticed for the first time his ankle was raw. I would check over the footage when I got home to see what he was up to.

"You said that already," I replied dryly. "When you were a part of the network"—I steeled myself for the flood of memories sure to come—"who was the person running the girls in this state?"

"I don't even know where the fuck we are, bitch." Alec had laid back down, folding his scrawny arms over his eyes to shield them from the light.

When I had finally tracked him down in New York, my teams smuggled him across state lines in a transport truck with an IV drip filled with a sedative strong enough for an elephant. I filled his living hours with light and kept him in the dark on everything else.

"Sequoia. Who was running the delivery service?"

I was kicking myself for not asking this question sooner. I was used to knowing every part of my domain, down to the most minute details, but my concern at the time hadn't been the West Coast; my focus had been honed in on the entire Eastern Seaboard in my vengeful search for justice.

That had been the birth of my crusade, the death of many perpetrators. Years later, here I stood.

My scouring search had been successful—it brought many to me before I finally found Alec, but my vengeful yearning remained. No amount of wrath-filled punishment on the scourge of our society ever took away the pain.

He remained mute. His sorry attempt at insubordination was a very unwise choice, given his position.

"Do you know why I haven't killed you, Alec?"

I dropped my voice, pressing against the glass hole and my venomous whisper carried over the vast emptiness of the clinical space.

"Death is too easy—too final. You will remain here until you fade away into nothingness. Your life will mean nothing. Your death will mean nothing. You. Are. Nothing."

I stood and tapped my red gloved fingers against the glass in veiled apathy. "But,"—I stared at my pretty red hands, the color mimicking the crimson palette of fresh blood—"I can make the nothingness easier. Perhaps I dim the lights one evening. I give you an extra bar another. Perhaps I get bored and put a bullet into your brain to end your suffering early."

My stare left my dancing fingers and zoomed in on Alec's pallid face as he watched me with cautious, sunken eyes. "I will give you the opportunity to choose your fate— the one thing you stole from *her*."

When the bitter word touched my tongue, I refused to taste it. Instead, I spat it out into the bright hallway and glared at my prisoner for forcing it into my mouth.

"The West Coast was owned by the Carlos Cartel," my captive admitted in a scratchy, hesitant drawl. "But the Midwest was Alvarez's territory."

"Which Alvarez?" My tone was sharp, viciously hungry for the truth of my situation. Each one of Alejandro's sons was his own brand of repulsive.

"Marco's."

The oldest brother. Marco appeared a white-collar family man; he ran two tech firms. How disgustingly fitting he'd trade tech by day and people by night.

"How long did he own the territory?"

A shrug of skin and bone. "As long as I was in the business. The trafficking was split up into four different zones, and whether the girls were international or domestic. He preferred to ship his girls in. I only dealt with domestic."

The vileness of this man, speaking of human beings as if they were products to be used and abused. If I wasn't so set on his suffering, I would kill him tonight.

"How many?" I swallowed my fear at the question, knowing the answer wouldn't be one I wanted to hear. But I had to hear it.

Alec's black eyes peered up into mine, their depths filled with an evil I'd never be able to name. His pink lips pouted upwards in an attempt at a smirk.

"Girls? A few thousand a year, maybe. Have to restock— not much of a lifespan in this line of work, is there?"

Remain calm, remain ... calm.

"You've chosen your fate."

I nodded to Joey, who moved aside, and input a passcode to unlock the tiny cupboard behind her. I removed a small slew of torture devices. An electric cattle prod, a bone saw, a handy pair of pliers. She'd get to choose her preferred method of torture tonight.

I would kill him in seconds if I conducted the torture session. I wasn't willing to let him go just yet.

"Make him bleed, but keep him alive. It'll have to be quick tonight. I'll be outside."

I forced my body to move at an unhurried pace, through the lit hallway and into the still-dark one, before stepping outside into the still night air of September.

I made it to my passenger door of the vehicle before my rage bubbled over into a spewing mass of pure hate. I couldn't contain it any longer; the acidic scream crept up from the roiling in my guts, and I slapped the metal skeleton with my open palm in bitter anguish.

My sobs dissipated into the dense tree line; immediately I clamped my mouth shut, and chastised myself for my lack of self-control in an area where avalanches were common.

I forced filling breaths of air down my throat and into my belly as I waited for Joey to return. All of my pretense was out the window – I needed to get a hold of myself before I made a crucial mistake.

I counted down from one thousand to clear my mind from the plaguing spiral of sorrow and got to 323 by the time Joey came out of the building. I walked over to the panel and reset the code using my slew of biometric software. Then we slipped back into the night, driving the dark, twisted road back toward home.

The next day came and went in a blur and my preplanned evening to myself was not going well. A few hours of trash television and a particularly back-breaking workout did nothing to assuage my feelings of guilt. Nor had an entire bottle of Champagne.

A visit with the demons of my past always made me restless and hungry for a distraction. I'd wallowed enough; I needed something in the present to ground me. To take me away from thoughts of *her*.

Sex was the perfect antidote.

Sex required no thought, no emotion, only *action*.

Sex had stopped being a connection of souls a decade ago; instead, I had molded the act into the perfect escape—a delicious release of pleasure and pain, an untethered bliss of in-the-moment relief.

It was a give-and-take of power and control. A mutually subscribed understanding—and occasionally, a subtle and effective weapon.

And, of course, I liked to come. Who didn't?

Kellan was still on my shit list, and I wouldn't be the one to grovel with Aaron. When he was ready to be tamed by a wanting woman and stone cold sober, he could come to me.

He'd left the next morning, just as I knew he would. I wouldn't be entertaining the whims of a sloppy man who couldn't commit to any path.

Not Aaron—not with the history we had.

Which left only one other man on my list. Marty had forwarded Lauchlan's contact information last week; I hadn't yet bothered to reach out.

Now that I knew the playing field, I was ready to play the game. How far would Lucky go to keep up the ruse? It was time for a little test.

I scrolled through my phone and typed a quick message with my name and my address. If Lauchlan was too stupid to recognize the booty call, then he certainly wouldn't be the man to satisfy me tonight, and I would have to find another way to test his resolve.

I was done feeling sorry for myself. Tomorrow, I would continue my quest to rid the world of despicable fucks like Marco Alvarez and Antonio Carlos. Tonight, I would indulge in the best escape known to woman.

I rose from my slump on the couch. From my walk-in closet, I selected the perfect set of lingerie.

It was time to get lucky.

CHAPTER 12

Lauchlan

I whistled a tune as I strolled through the hallways of Ma's penthouse suite, heading for the shower to clean up from a hell of a day. Bossing techies around was a bit of a bore, so I was itching to get out in the field to do my real job.

I stood under the hot spray and lost myself to the ritual of soap, grooming, a good tug from thoughts of another shower experience, and a thorough rinse, before getting out to see a flashing notification on my phone.

Unknown: Hillary. 5767 Rodham Drive, Penthouse A. Code 746.

Still sopping wet, I froze and read the text three more times, squinting my eyes at the screen to make sure my brain hadn't melted in the shower.

The cheeky little minx.

In my line of work, I rubbed shoulders with powerful men and women alike, but Blondie had an essence about her—a fierce commander in a tight dress and sex heels. And fuck me if it didn't make my dick jump every time I thought about her.

You can command me to your heart's content, Mo Mhuirnin.

A text at near midnight could only be one of two things: I was about to get offed, or fucked. I would always take the risk where little Blondie was concerned.

I changed quickly into dark jeans and a light Henley, not wasting a second, in case this text was coming from a moment of weakness. I was an opportunistic cunt at the best of times, and I wasn't passing up the chance for an evening between a beautiful woman's thighs.

And to see her penthouse, of course. Couldn't think of a better way to get into her fortress than through a little foreplay. This was turning out to be a banner day, after all.

My cock stiffened to half-mast as I imagined how she'd taste. Christ, I was turning into a right fifteen-year-old virgin.

I made my way down ten stories, but then reconsidered using a vehicle and walked across the park instead.

The Tallaght streets of Dublin had raised me, and a light jog across the fancy park in Carlisle's downtown before midnight was practically a child's playground in school hours. I hadn't strapped on my gun or knife. I had no intentions of keeping my clothes on, and my accessories weren't a topic of conversation I was interested in having tonight.

I was hoping to do no talking at all.

Picturing my Blondie with a thigh strap holding a sheath of daggers took all the blood from my system right to the head of my dick.

I took a deep breath and rode the glitzy lift to her floor, centering myself and my teenage cock. Her building was far fancier than Ma's, but none of that mattered to me. You see one gorgeous building, you've seen them all. I preferred to look at art or jewelry, or beautiful people. They had far better stories to tell.

I cared about the security system. I subtly glanced at the mirrored walls, catching two cameras and a motion sensor just above the door. Pretty typical for a condo—Blondie must be smarter than that.

The lift took me right into her place; the doors opened into a stark foyer. I peered around the space, but didn't hear a soul.

My adrenaline spiked at the thought of a little adult game of naked 'hide-and-seek.' Or cat-and-mouse murder.

No matter, really – I could kill a man with my bare hands if need be.

Messy stuff, though. I much preferred sex.

I quickly assessed the entry, seeking more cameras and motion sensors. I took out my phone to do a micro scan, detecting the five visible and three hidden pieces of hardware. Once they were all cataloged, I shoved my phone back into my jeans and said every prayer to the Celtic gods, hoping this was about to be the booty call of my dreams.

Before I could lean into the thrill of a good chase, I turned the corner to find my hostess waiting for me. She sat on the couch in the open living room, wearing nothing but a deep pink corset and panties. A set of sheer silver tights were clipped to a sassy little garter belt at the tops of her thighs. A silky robe hung loosely around her shoulders, and she languidly slouched back against the arm of the couch. She stared at me with the blaze of a challenge in her eyes.

Fuck, the spell of this woman. I cast my eyes upward for the briefest of seconds.

Thank you, Epona, for the pleasure I'm about to receive.

"Lucky," she crooned, before taking a slow pull of a glass of white wine. She gestured to the seat beside her on the white leather couch. "Take a seat."

My feet obeyed long before my head did; I removed my boots and leather jacket, eyeing the crystal glass of dark liquid waiting on the coffee table in front of her.

I cradled the glass as I settled in beside her, inhaling the scent of my favorite whiskey.

"You're quite the hostess, Blondie."

A manic grin took over her features; I knew it well—the face of someone who had a fire of energy trapped inside their blood, desperate to release it. The kind of high you couldn't get from any drug, but from taking something from someone else.

What had she been up to before she summoned my muscled arse? A ruthless takeover? A hostile coup?

I didn't care, as long as she worked that energy out on me.

I'll take your sins, sweetie.

"Are you up for a little game, Lauchlan?"

My name was pointed on her lethal little tongue. She was goading me; I liked it.

"I'm always up for a little game, Blondie." I pursed my lips into a smirk and winked before tipping the glass and drinking the amber liquid in one go; the delicious burn heated my insides to the point of no pain.

"I've got a little toy chest over there." She nodded toward a heavy-looking silver box at the end of the table. "Open it."

Curiosity outweighed my impulse to defy the command; I shifted my weight and pulled the box toward me, unclipping the delicate fastening to seek its treasure like the horny pirate I was.

My eyes widened as I sifted through the contents. Organized like an oversized fishing tackle box, it had colorful bits and bobs in neat rows. A vibrating butt plug the size of my fist, with a jewel knob on the end. A clit suction thing I had never seen before. Countless dildos in all shapes and sizes, and a two-pronged penis poker strap-on.

I whistled through my teeth, impressed at the assortment of toys. Hillary was into some kinky shyte.

"I don't do collars or handcuffs, Blondie." I bit my lip as my gaze wandered her body. Her legs had opened, revealing a damp strip of silk over her cunt—and nipples hard as pebbles against the lace of her lingerie.

She was as horny as I was; I'd bet my last dollar she was at the edge of her control too.

"I already have someone for that." She waved a hand dismissively, quirking another eyebrow at me in challenge. "Choose one. Or two. I like variety, as you can see."

I loved the deviant defiance in her eyes. Taunting me into the submission she wanted. Fucking this woman would be the most fun sex of my life, I was sure of it.

"That one is my favorite."

A red-tipped nail pointed to the purple pegging toy with two veiny penises at either end.

The cheeky *minx*. I loved a saucy woman, but Hillary Lane took it to an entirely new level.

I stared back at her, not breaking eye contact and meeting her challenge as I pulled it out of the box. I grabbed the bottle of lube next to it, holding the toy up in a taunt of my own.

"A two-in-one. You want to spoon me, Blondie? Drive a dick into my arse?"

I caught the barest flicker of surprise in her eyes, but she recovered so fast a less trained person would have missed it.

Good. She could play with me all she wanted; I was a willing participant if it meant I could have a sweet taste of her perfect wet cunt.

The lengths I was willing to go for a job. Such sacrifices.

Hillary slowly picked herself off of the couch, revealing the delicate nuances of her outfit. Small but perky breasts, large nipples I couldn't wait to suck on, wide hips I could grab as I fucked her hard and fast. Round ass cheeks I'd bite until they were marked as mine.

She wasn't just trim, she was toned. Muscular, for a small woman, even if she was one of those bloody annoying health nuts.

When she took the pegger and lube out of my hands, I caught a whiff of delicate perfume. Jasmine and... rose. Expensive and enticing.

"Take your pants off."

No one could say I wasn't a dedicated man on a mission. I was about to have a silicon cock up my arse to keep up my pretense, but if getting fucked by a beautiful woman was a sacrifice I'd have to make, call me a goat and throw me on the altar.

Fill me up, Blondie.

I tilted my head up to stare into those baby blues and sank deeper into the couch, opening my arms wide across the back of it. "Take them off for me."

She tutted disapprovingly but I matched her stare, ready to play her games, but not as her hand puppet. She set the toys on the table in front of her and moved into my space, placing her hands on either side of my neck. Her soft fingers lay warm against my skin.

"I had a feeling you were going to be difficult, Lucky."

I snorted—there was no chance this woman took home patsies to play with.

She rested her thighs on either side of mine, and pushed upward to press her breasts into my face. I mouthed at one nipple through the pink lace, tasting the salt of her skin through the fabric. She shuddered against me and I moved to the other breast, soaking the mound with my tongue.

"Lucky for you, I like difficult men." She dropped her weight into my lap and ground her clit against the solid steel of my shaft. We groaned together and her soft pants against my ear spurred me into a frenzy. I grasped her waist tightly to stop her from grinding against me again.

"I'd rather you come on my tongue, Blondie. Don't waste that sweet sticky mess on my jeans."

I nipped the bottom of her earlobe, kissing the underside of her jaw and moving to the sensitive patch of muscle at the base of her neck to her shoulder. I latched my tongue over the spot and sucked hard, still holding her in place against me. She wriggled, trying to get some friction, but my hold was too strong. I smiled against her skin when she moaned a satisfying combination of lust and frustration.

"Take them off for me," I repeated. Shifting her off my lap and depositing her on the cushion beside me, I stood. My cock pushed painfully against my zipper. I pulled up the hem of my Henley. I tapped the metal button at the stitching on my jeans.

"Start here."

Her eyes blazed, but she obeyed. I swallowed a chuckle and watched her take her sweet time unbuttoning and unzipping my pants. She shucked them down my legs, along with my boxers in one go. My cock sprung free, hovering in the small space between us.

I'd had to settle into some pretty compromising positions to get a job done—once with a 300-pound Russian man who thankfully liked to be tied up—but I'd never *enjoyed* myself this much in the process.

My Celtic goddess, Epona, got the shout out tonight, but so did the greedy git who'd hired me.

"A taste for a taste?" I palmed my erection and spread the pre-cum drop on the cupid's bow of her lips. She licked the wee bead off with her tongue, and it stirred the mangy mutt inside me.

"You can rail me as hard as you want, Blondie, but I'm having a taste of your cunt before you do."

I kicked my pants behind the coffee table, then knelt in front of her. Dragging her hips toward me, the sharp, sweet smell of her arousal hit me like a wave and made my mouth water.

I snapped the tiny lace strap of her thong with a well-placed tug and buried my face between her thighs, spearing my tongue into her slick cunt. Even her pre-cum tasted rich —as if high-tiered geneticists had created a sweeter cocktail —I was drinking her elixir until there was nothing left.

I ate her with enthusiasm and years of practice, my lips and tongue pulling every depraved sound from her mouth like she was made for sexual conquest. I moved to her clit, sucking rapidly until her thighs tightened around my ears and her whole body stiffened as she let out a cry that made my dick want to shed its tears and release.

I wiped my mouth against her soft flesh and left a small bite before moving again to stand. I pulled my Henley over my head. Body fully naked, my weeping cock begged for attention.

Her dazed gaze only lasted seconds before she rolled to the side and off the couch faster than I would have given her credit. She reached for the toys on the table and pushed me, face forward, into the back of the couch.

"Your turn."

I chuckled into the soft material as I felt her move behind me. I gripped the back of the couch, waiting for the cool silk of lube to fill my ass crack. She didn't disappoint—in seconds I was coated and she slid a soft finger into my hole.

I shivered from the pleasure when she hooked her fingers, hitting my prostate over and over until I was on the cliff of coming.

"What are you waiting for, Blondie?" I taunted on a grunt when she hit that tasty little button once more. "Don't tell me you're going to miss the chance to rail me. Fuck me like you mean it."

When she removed her fingers, a moment later I felt the light pressure of lubed silicone against my arse. The two dicks were opposite ends, so one would be in me. The other would fill her cunt. She'd fuck us both into oblivion. As far as being dominated went, this was the best-case scenario dreams were made of.

But fuck me, woman, get on with it. I was so tense my dick was about to fall off.

Without a warning, she drove deep into me. When her pelvis hit the back of my cheeks, she paused, and a low, vibrating pulse filled me, shooting sparks across my vision and right through the tip of my about-to-explode dick.

"Fuck, Blondie," I spit out through gritted teeth. "Stop teasin' me. Give me the good stuff."

Whether she was done with her own torture or willing to play ball, I didn't care. She reached around and squeezed my shaft up and down as she drove into me, again and again, upping the vibrations as we grunted and panted and groaned and –

"Fuck!" Tingles shot up my spine. I reached for my Henley just in time to capture the stream of cum; she let out a voracious cry behind me.

We collapsed against the couch, her front to my back. The toy remained deeply seated inside of both of us as we caught our breaths.

Her cum leaked out on my arse cheeks, and out around the toy. I looked forward to feeling her cum around my cock as I flooded her pussy with my own.

Next time. There would most definitely be a next time. I could keep up the ruse as long as necessary to experience her cunt in a few more ways.

Eventually, she pulled out of me and stood, dropping the sticky toy onto the table. I rolled over and lazily watched her walk down the hallway to presumably clean up. Her lingerie was rightly askew, and I watched her appled arse cheeks with interest as she left.

Next time, I was going to be the one sliding in between those cheeks.

When she didn't return five minutes later, I sighed and got dressed, grateful I had captured my cum on the inside of my shirt so I could do my walk of shame without the evidence of it on full display.

Walk of triumph, more like. There was no shame here tonight.

When she still hadn't come out ten minutes later, I put on my boots and coat and left, effectively dismissed from the best booty call I'd ever had.

In my line of work, I was rarely surprised, but I had to be prepared for everything. Tonight, I had been totally surprised and completely unprepared by how much I liked it. That thrill itself was addictive, let alone the earth-shattering fuck.

A billionaire businesswoman had just pegged the shit out of me. And fuck me, I hoped she did it again.

"I don't like your approach on this one."

Marcia Donavon, my Ma and technical boss, tapped her fingers on the glass like she was irritated with me, then ignored me by looking out into the traffic several stories below.

She'd been here too long, her Irish accent muted with American twang. American twang wasn't a bad thing—personally, I found the accent sexy—on anyone but my mother—but the lack of Gaelic dialect on her tongue made me a wee bit nostalgic.

Odd, given I hadn't lived with Ma in twenty years.

I was used to her underestimating me. I shrugged and settled into the wraparound couch in the center of the living room.

"My approach is working just fine, Ma. Got some bite marks to prove it."

That took her eyes off the buggered cars. She shot me a disapproving glower, which made me smirk even more. Marcia may be renowned in these circles, but so was I. I knew what I was doing.

"She doesn't need an Alpha, Ma. She needs a nice willing Beta who can surprise her every once in a while." I winked and swung my boots up to rest on the coffee table.

"Lauch." Ma pinched the bridge of her nose as if in pain and came to sit across from me in her expensive Norwegian chair. Where Ma worked this life for fancy furniture and status, I did it for the thrill.

Adrenaline was my favorite drug of choice. A good fuck, a close second. Thoughts of Hillary's smooth and supple body riding my cock like she wanted to strangle it slid into my mind, and I casually held my hand over my swelling dick. Didn't want to have a chub in front of Ma. Goddamn embarrassing.

"This requires delicate handling. This isn't just a job—there are a lot of close ties there to the Carlos Cartel. Your arrogance could get you killed."

She stared at me hard, like I was a roll of cellophane wrapping. Apparently, I wasn't trembling enough in my boots.

"For fuck's sake, take this seriously!"

I swung my legs back down, rested my elbows on my knees and plastered the most serious face I could muster—one I had practiced in the mirror a time or two.

"Ma," I crooned gently, "trust me on this one. You've built your legacy, and so have I. Give me a few months. I won't be stuck somewhere for years and then come out empty-handed."

She bristled at the insinuation, but I couldn't help slipping the wee barb in there. Years ago, she'd worked a long con that went sideways. Her target went to jail, and she lost out on some serious loot.

To say The Six weren't happy was like saying I loved a good rail up the arse—understatement of the century. Da was sure they'd strip her of her title and send her packing, but they'd given her a second chance. She'd worked bloody hard to clear her name since then.

To the rest of the world, Ol' Marcie was in 'tech', made millions doing it, and had a wide network of filthy rich contacts all across the state. To The Six, she was one of their lead 'acquisition agents', a pretty little title for 'thieving con artist', and had built a reputation all over the world for 'acquiring' things.

When Da died, I had a choice; take over his spot in the European chapter, or come to America and give it a go. I'd never been to this side of the pond, and the call of adventure was sweet music to my ears.

Jobs in Europe were too ... typical. Art, jewels, some king of an ancient dynasty no one cared about. But in America...

Tech moguls. Stock market billions. The land of excess. More deals, more thrills. Ironic I was sent to America for a European goldmine, but life had a funny way of working out, sometimes. When Bellamy handed me Hillary's picture as my next job, I knew it would be the con of a lifetime. The beautiful, sassy woman would be the ultimate egg to crack. And I was a wicked good cook.

I'd needed a cover reason to come to America for years, and my goddess handed me one - for all my good behaviour, likely.

And cartels? A dime a dozen. Sure, big scary brutes with machine guns weren't my favorite thing, but I'd be long gone before a cartel baddie could get a hold of me. I hadn't earned the title 'Shadow' by being a slow git.

And if they did? Well, Kellan Carlos wouldn't be a problem. I had a plan to make sure of it.

Being closer to Ma was another push. She'd visited a few times a year throughout my wee years, but we'd never had a *bond* or anything. With Da gone, I figured it was time to do my duty to the last of the family. At least I could reassure her of this.

"I'm already in her bed, Ma. Trust I know what I'm doing."

She released a pent-up sigh and shook her head in irritation, but my answer must have satisfied her somewhat, because the fire under her arse disappeared.

"No slip-ups. This could be the gig that makes us; don't fuck it up for the sake of your dick."

"I'll have you know that my dick is a true gentleman," I lied, moving to make myself a sandwich in the kitchen. "But you don't need to worry, Ma. Our beautiful Blondie doesn't suspect a thing."

I grinned to myself as I perfectly grilled a butty for breakfast. This just might be the most fun job yet.

CHAPTER 13

Kellan

"Fold."

Mical threw the playing cards onto the poker table in disgust, his bitter sneer pulling at the jagged scar down the side of his face and into his black hairline.

It was a recent wound; a ballsy fucker had sliced a knife through his cheek in a dispute over territory in Cascade Falls. The territory I handed to my brothers six years ago.

I'd made the trek down to their base of operations in Sheldonville, in the jazz club our dead brother had built up as the crux of his empire. They'd done nothing to change it in the years since—green velvet curtains and dark wood surrounded us like we were Al Capone and Lucky Luciano at the height of their heyday.

Fitting, since the building was once used for rum running during Prohibition. Though, the items in the bowels of today's basement cellar were far more dangerous than pints of country swill alcohol.

"*Que Cabron*," Jonah muttered darkly as he threw his cards into the pile in the center of the table.

I laughed and pulled the hundreds of dollars worth of chips toward me. "Jonah, you could have called me. You just lost five hundred for nothing."

His coal-black eyes stared viciously back at me. "You have pocket aces," he spat. "Do not bullshit me, brother."

I grinned and stacked the chips into tidy piles while Mical scrolled through his phone, angry snarl still firmly in place.

My older twin half brothers were opportunistic, sadistic bastards; cheating them at cards was my favorite way to piss them off before a meeting with our father. A way to remind them of the chain of command.

A few rounds of Texas Hold 'Em was our ritual to cut a bit of tension before Antonio laid out his expectations for his dutiful sons.

I had never been close with any of my brothers; we were all bastard children of different mothers our father had handpicked to be the successors of his empire. When the twins relocated to Sequoia County to take over one side of the operations, we'd formed an alliance, if not a bond.

The twins were half-Israeli, half-Columbian, their matching dark hair, dark eyes, and bronze skin still mirror images of each other despite being in their forties. I was the product of a Swedish mother and Antonio's Columbian blood. We looked nothing alike, blessed with our mothers' genes instead of our brutal father, but our shared upbringing had honed us into unforgiving weapons of brutality.

Two of my brothers were dead. Another was safely tucked away—Antonio wasn't aware of his existence, and I planned to keep it that way. The three of us were all that remained of the next generation of cartel criminals. A double agent and two ruthless assholes.

The men sitting in front of me didn't possess a conscience. They didn't carry the same narcissism our father did; they didn't care about anything at all. Everyone in their path was a means to an end. Antonio ordered, and they delivered. Mindless, murdering sycophants.

I wasn't stupid enough to turn my back to them.

I checked my watch. Antonio was meticulously on time and would arrive in five minutes. I needed to speak with my brothers quickly.

I knocked on the rich lacquered wood of the table's trim. Mical looked up with familiar irritation, but he put his phone down.

"The tides are changing in Sequoia." I nodded to Mical's scar and leveled my stare at the two of them. "The Carlos Cartel is being challenged."

Jonah shrugged one rounded shoulder, the muscles bulging beneath his tight dark shirt. "We are always being challenged. Today is no different."

"Perhaps," I agreed, thinking of the many stooges armed with handguns and shit-for-brains who had tried to take on the family in the past. The dead man who'd carved into Mical's face was the exception. "But I keep hearing whispers of Alejandro Alvarez in our territory. Have you heard this?"

Jonah's careful mask of indifference slid over his harsh features, but he said nothing. He was notoriously calculating and gave nothing away without a trade—but by his body language alone, I knew he'd at least heard the rumors.

Mical was far less controlled. His dark eyes glittered with malice and a vicious grin took over his face. "What will you trade in return, brother? I could use a favor from the next heir."

I grunted in response, in no mood to discuss the inevitable shift of our posts in the coming months. Killing my brother had come at a very heavy price. I was now his replacement to take over the family throne. In the many years of toeing the line, I had never wanted to be king.

I glanced at my watch again. One minute.

"We'll discuss this later." I glared at them pointedly. Alvarez was a threat that needed to be eliminated, and it would be far cleaner to rid him on our side of things before the FBI or DEA got involved.

We were the devil the authorities knew. I couldn't risk our usefulness—it was the only reason I had walked the line for so long. Trish only had so much power.

The twins immediately stood stiffly to attention, and I knew Antonio and his men must have entered the room behind me.

I stood and turned to greet the man who had crafted us in his image, dipping my head in a respectful nod. The dignified seventy-year-old with tanned skin and silver hair strode to greet us. Three of his heavily armed, most trusted men marched in, taking positions by his side.

It was pretty telling that Antonio Carlos, leader of the largest cartel on this side of the continent, brought his guards to a meeting with his sons. Family was as likely to turn on you as your enemies in our world. If I thought it was possible, I would have killed him long ago.

"*Hijo,*" Antonio rasped with a commanding timbre as he reached out to wrap me in a perfunctory hug. "It has been too long."

Before I could respond, he moved on to my brothers. I took the moment to assess the men he'd chosen to bring to our meeting today.

Manuel and Soloman, the two had stuck by Antonio's side since I was a teenager. The third man was unfamiliar to me. A bald man with gold hoops in his ears and blank green eyes—the same kind of face of a serial killer on America's Most Wanted.

I shifted my focus back to my father, making a mental note to scan the new man's profile later.

Antonio Carlos beckoned with the spindly fingers of a man used to holding all the power in a room.

"Sit."

I did as he asked, shifting my weight to fit into the small leather loveseat to my right, while Jonah and Mical sat in the armchairs on either side of the small seating area. A heavy silence settled over us as we waited expectantly for Antonio to start the family meeting.

"It has been too long," he repeated. The shrewd man's dark expression narrowed in on me as he scanned every facet of my face. He always did this when we met in person —as if he could determine my allegiance by a simple review of the tightness of my skin.

I had betrayed him once, and he'd spared my life, but only because the betrayal had handed him a line of security —a double agent he could manipulate instead of a son he would protect.

The moment I failed to be useful was the moment I would die.

I stared back into his piercing gaze, refusing to cower in his presence. Despite the thousands of men he'd killed in cold blood over decades of commanding an underground army, the man didn't scare me. His involvement in my life was a necessary evil, as were my brothers.

A small crinkle in his left eye told me he was satisfied with what he saw, his attention turning to the two nitwits instead.

"It would seem you have been busy, Mical." Antonio nodded toward the jagged line cutting Mical's cheek in half. "Is he now dead?"

"Yes." Mical spat on the pristine cream carpet in disgust like a child. "And he suffered greatly."

"And his family?"

"Also dead." Jonah spoke up in a hollow voice of disinterested detachment. "They will no longer be an issue for us."

Antonio nodded his head in approval. "And the fights?"

"Successful. There are now seventeen separate clubs across five states, each taking in over a million in bets a month." Jonah continued in his clipped, emotionless tone. "Washing is going well—we're cleaning half of what we're bringing in on a weekly basis through hundreds of channels."

"Good. Mical?"

"Product is moving faster than we can supply it. Demand is heavy. We have another facility up and running in Venezuela, with three alternative shipping routes. The dope is selling faster than coke, so we're dusting our other products to increase the demand of those product lines."

Fuckers. I'd tip Trish off about one of our favored routes and get the tainted fentanyl off the streets, but it wouldn't be enough. I'd have to keep the Venezuela warehouse under my hat for now—but I could get one of the other warehouses in Columbia taken down to help balance the scales for a little while.

When one cockroach was crushed into dust, another skittered in to take its place. The cat-and-mouse game with my family was the price my soul paid for my life being spared all those years ago. I led the enemy, spied for the opposition, and sold out both parties when the need arose. The price of my life wasn't worth the reward.

Our soulless leader clucked his tongue in approval. "And the guns?"

"Three new large buyers in the west. Shipping out fresh boxes next week, once the Russians can get their supply off the ground."

They were opportunistic shits, but my brothers weren't dumb. Their side of the business brought in hundreds of millions of dollars to the Cartel a year, even after they'd left their post in California to take over Sequoia's operations.

"Have you noticed any supplies missing?" I carefully worded my question, not ready to give Antonio any sign of Alvarez moving into our towns. It was possible he already knew, and I couldn't add another 'task' to my already very full plate.

"No." Mical's retort was short and angry, as per usual. "Nothing missing. Our men care too much for their heads to steal from us."

"Why do you ask, *mijo*?"

"Work." I kept my answer succinct. "Rumblings of a new weapon supplier. I'm working on it."

Antonio nodded swiftly, then shifted his focus to *my* businesses.

"And what do you have for me?"

The simple question was as dangerous as an AK-47 in the hands of a crazed fucker on meth. I squared my shoulders and leveled my gaze at my father.

"I am in Carlisle investigating a major theft ring. Purely white collar, nothing to do with the Cartel or its players. Our partners are complying and paying their tithes on time. The Rodriguezes plan to open up three more brothels in the next year—they are becoming quite lucrative."

"Good." My father answered smoothly; with the precision of his pitch, I knew something else would follow— something I would not like in the least.

"Increase their tithe. If they want to continue in the sex trade, they will pay us more for the pleasure. Which brings me to my next concern."

His eyes narrowed to slits, and his veiled discontent crept quietly to the surface of his skin.

"You are not doing enough, *mijo*. Keeping the FBI off our back and feeding them our enemies in return is not enough in these trying times. I am getting old and tired. Our girls need to be overseen—guided. You will take over this side of the business."

'Girls' as in the women torn from the streets, drugged, and shipped out to be sold to the highest bidders. The rest were chained in brothels until they died from a sexual disease or an overdose. It was the most disgusting revenue stream of the family business, and I had vehemently spoken out against it since I was old enough to know the difference.

He was finally punishing me for the death of my brother by handing me the one thing I hated most in this world.

Gangbangers chose this life. They took the risk for the promise of high reward, and it was their right to choose the way they died. Stolen women sold into a life of sexual slavery was depravity the devil himself wouldn't take part in.

"No." Antonio Carlos did not hear the word often. He broke into a dark smile while his eyes betrayed his fury.

"You do not have the luxury to say no. Your duty is to this family, and your life debt is to *me*. Or is your life no longer of value?"

Mical grinned with vicious delight and Jonah's mask cracked just a fraction. No love was lost between us; my death would mean more power and attention for them.

"I am more valuable to you alive than dead." I folded my arms across my broad chest and stared into the soulless black depths of his gaze. "The operation is too large for me to oversee and maintain my position. Do you prefer I spend my time eliminating your enemies or coddling your *putas*? Which has more value to you?"

A tremulous silence fell over the space as my father held my glare. I didn't miss the quiet click of the safety being released against a metal gun barrel behind me. His men waited for his signal for permission to put a bullet into my brain and be done with my insolence.

"This is why you will become king." Antonio stood gracefully from his seat and pulled my cheeks between his palms.

"You are brave, *mijo,* but do not mistake stupidity for bravery again. You have until January. Then the *putas* will very much be your concern."

He signaled behind me; shuffling feet and the opening of the heavy wooden door broke through the heavy stillness as his cronies cleared the hallway for them to leave.

"Do not disappoint me, Kellan." His hardened expression said everything his mouth wasn't. January or death. No other option. He turned his attention to my brother. "Fix your face, Mical. You look like a Russian."

Flames of fiery acid burned through my gut as my father casually walked away from handing me a death sentence.

"My money is on the *putas*." Mical snickered as he and Jonah followed behind, leaving me alone to wrestle with my fate in peace.

CHAPTER 14

Hillary

I tumbled down the well in billowing skirts, my hair whipping around me on a strange, floaty breeze. I landed in the center of the earth; the land where my nightmares lived and forced me to play.

I hit the hard ground with a hard thump, but I didn't feel any pain. The pain down here wasn't physical—even when I was speared to death, or had my hair pulled out by its roots, I couldn't actually sense it; this place was a mental torture chamber, a rolling display of all my past failures and those yet to come.

The familiar resounding sound of horse hooves racing toward me reverberated in my bones, and I braced myself for him.

A disjointed laugh echoed all around me as the black stallion stopped in my path, its rider cloaked in shadows. The bronze skeleton mask molded to his face hiding his features, but I knew it was him. It was always him.

"Are you lost, little girl?"

The dark resonance of his voice was soothing; coaxing me into a false sense of calm. I wrinkled my brow in confusion, looking down at my appearance to see what he saw. Who I appeared to be this time.

I wore a baby pink nightgown with white teddy bears stitched across the front; pretty hand-darned laced cuffs covered the lengths of my forearms; an exact replica of the one my grandmother had gifted me when I was five.

I shook my head at the rider and cast my gaze downward, clutching the soft blue stuffed toy elephant in my fist. I hadn't even realized I'd been holding it.

"Come."

The rider beckoned me forward with a leather-gloved hand, and I felt an inexplicable pull toward him. He swiftly hopped down from his horse and placed two rough hands on my hips before lifting me onto the front of his saddle. I complied and said nothing, as if my ability to fight had somehow been taken from me.

I shivered, but not from cold. He pulled himself up and settled behind me. Grabbing the reins, he commanded the horse forward. Tears fell down my cheeks in a constant drip as we took off at a steady pace, traveling through a landscape of nothing but blackness.

The terrain changed; we hovered on the bank of a blood-red river, human-shaped shadows floating on top of the sluggish water. Wisps of hands reached for me, their anguished voices muffled by the burble and bubble of the liquid all around us.

His firm body loomed over me and his mouth hovered beside my ear. His gentle whisper was delivered softly, but the message hardened every vein in my body to ice.

"You see, little girl? It's not so bad in the dark."

I woke with a start, a sheen of sweat coating my limbs like a second skin. Tremors wracked through my body as I came down from the dream.

I wasn't supposed to dream. The strong prescription sedative I took every night should knock out every thought from my exhausted brain, but every now and again, a slew of nightmares slipped through like trained warriors of terror.

Tonight's dream had been different. I had never shown up as a child before—I was usually college age when the rider appeared to take me away. My visit with Alec was influencing me more than I thought.

I removed my eye mask and pulled out my noise-canceling ear plugs, using the sounds of my bedroom as a distraction to calm my heart rate.

The steady hum of the mechanical cooling system—breath—the faint beep of my security system at the elevator—breath—the drip of the faucet in my ensuite that I still hadn't gotten fixed—breath.

Five minutes of sound meditation brought me back down to earth. I was in my bedroom, lying in my California King, under the softest duvet known to man, in the most secure building in the city.

Logic wasn't enough. My mind kept dredging up memories I had spent years compartmentalizing. I needed a distraction.

I couldn't scroll through my phone; news of more criminals, election candidates, and business stats would kick-start my brain into work mode, and I didn't need that at—I looked at my phone for the time—3:30 a.m.

Fuck. I was many things, but an early morning riser was *not* one of them.

One thing always helped, but I hated using it. I couldn't remember the last time I'd needed it. My hesitation to send the text was a bitter battle between my pride and my desperate desire for a few more hours of sleep.

Sleep won. I sent off the message before I could convince myself it wasn't worth the inconvenience, then threw my phone into my covers before I gave in to the sucking spiral of social media.

I regretted that decision immediately. Within moments, my phone buzzed from somewhere in the duvet, and I had to hunt through the pile of pillowy feathers to fish it out.

"Hey," I answered, keeping my voice quiet even though I was completely alone in the condo.

"Hey, Hill."

Logan's normally arrogant tenor was soft, and I immediately regretted reaching out to him. He had a whole family at home; they all slept in the same room most nights.

"I'm sorry I woke you."

"You didn't. It's my turn with Noble tonight. I'm rocking this little monster back to sleep."

The image alone was enough to make me smile. We'd known each other our entire lives; had lived together, slept together, waged war against our fathers together. In all that time, I never could have imagined he'd play the doting father. Perhaps because I could never imagine myself as a mother. Time and circumstances had changed him.

Despite going our separate ways, he had become one of my dearest friends. I was his sobriety partner and helped him beat his addictions. He had given me the evidence to send our fathers to prison; although Stanley had disappeared without a trace, and Camden was living the high life under house arrest. Our lives intertwined in an irrevocable way.

He didn't know about my vendetta, or the events that made my vendetta the beating thrum of my heart. But he knew me.

"How are you?"

I heard a shift as he adjusted the phone to his ear.

"Really, Hill?" His familiar conceited tone came through my speaker despite its quiet delivery. I could picture the haughty raise of his dark brows and the self-satisfied smirk, a look I'd seen a million times. "You're going to have a catch-up call *now*?"

I ignored him. "How are the cravings?"

A long-suffering sigh blew into the phone, followed by a second of silence.

"The cravings are fine, Hill. Still in NA, still staying away from everything I need to. Winter's doing better, Noble's fine. Hell, the guys are also fine, and I even like Shane some days."

Before I could get the chance to ask another time-delaying question, he spoke again. "Okay, great catch-up. Tell me about the nightmare."

"I didn't say anything about a nightmare."

"You text me in the middle of the night three times a year and it's always about a nightmare. Winter's going to be upset you're not telling her about this, you know."

I slumped further into my bed and pulled the covers over me into a cozy cocoon. I pulled on my eye mask while I considered how to answer him.

"I don't tell Winter because she'll worry. You don't worry about me."

"Mostly true," he agreed. "But its gotta be some fucking nightmare if you're using *me* as your distraction. What gives, Hill?"

I closed my eyes and described the nightmare in detail, down to the very last ghost of a human trying to grab hold of the rider's horse.

Logan let out a low whistle, before muttering "shit, sorry buddy" when Noble let out a startled cry.

"Sounds like the nightmares I had in withdrawal. Winter sleeping next to me helped. Maybe you need a cuddle buddy." He let out an irritated huff. "Fuck, I sound like Shane."

I snorted into my pillow. "I can't sleep next to anyone. A cuddle buddy will *not* help."

"You slept next to me." He laughed before I could get the words out. "Yeah, I know, we definitely weren't cuddling. You made sure there were three feet between us at all times. But you have a huge bed in there, Hill. If the nightmares keep coming, try it. Probably isn't hard to find a man who wants to sleep with you."

"Maybe I'll get four, like you do." I teased back. The unorthodox lifestyle he'd chosen never failed to amuse me.

"Not as bad as it sounds, actually." Logan let out a light chuckle. "I've got to go. Noble's finally asleep. I have a short window to get him down before he notices I'm missing."

I could feel my heart rate slowing, and my eyes getting heavier by the second. His advice was third tier at best, but our shared history had done its work to calm me back into a state of drowsiness.

"Thanks for calling," I whispered, grateful he'd bothered to get back to me at this late hour. His loyalty and friendship were as precious to me as his son was to him.

"Of course." I heard the soft click of a door and imagined him walking down the short hallway back to the master bedroom. I knew the layout well—it had originally been my house, after all.

"And Hill? Spend some of your billions on therapy. If a fucking shrink can help me, it can help anybody."

The soft click on the other side of the state was all I heard through the line. I slipped on my earphones, nestled into the safety of my blankets, and promptly fell to sleep.

"Marco, lovely to see you again."

The words were citrus to a raging canker sore on my tongue, but I maintained the professional smile I'd cemented to my lips.

He rose from his seat in the plush royal blue booth to shake my hand, an equally professional smile holding his cheeks in place. Pale gray eyes politely assessed me from the top of my curled blonde locks to the tips of my cream Louboutins.

I repressed a disgusted shudder at his attention.

I'd chosen Quintessence to talk business today. The familiar territory and common ground did little to assuage my nerves, but if all went to rot, Jeremy would have my back.

I scanned the bar as I settled into the comfortable booth seat, hoping for a glimpse of my favorite bartender. The crest of salt and pepper hair at the other end of the vast walnut bar-top settled my stomach only slightly, but I took the win.

Taming blood-thirsty sharks was a very routine part of conducting business at the top level of society; I was no stranger to swimming in their waters and leaving scarring bite marks when the situation called for it. Now that I knew the depths of Marco Alvarez's depravity, I wanted to shred him into tough, blubbery pieces and leave him as chum.

I was an equally honed predator, yet, I was still a woman, biologically programmed to sense danger in the air from a man who felt he owned me and my sisters. The high-pitched wail no one else could hear warned we owed *him* for the gift of his attention, and he would take it by whatever means necessary.

I was definitely not into *that* kind of primal play.

"Let's cut to the chase." Marco's slithering tenor slid over my skin like a poisonous snake. "Now that the Rodriguezes have joined our group of companies, you are no longer the power player. Shall we start making concessions now?"

Oh, ho. This was going to be fun.

"You mean, the elder Rodriguezes have joined your group of companies," I said. "You seem to be forgetting that I have the true brains behind the operation as my partner. Not to mention considerable backing from the state."

Marco's stare was unblinking, keeping his hands clasped in front of him as if my position was of no consequence.

"Veronica and Vicente are a force to be reckoned with." Pearly teeth flashed, an innocent smirk layered with malicious intent. "They have aligned themselves with a business they can trust."

Armed with our drinks, Jeremy's lean form stopped at our table.

What a saint.

I welcomed the interruption, and took a long sip of my dirty martini to tame the boiling tendrils of anger seeping through my blood. Marco accepted the crystal tumbler of what looked to be bourbon from Jeremy's outstretched hand, then turned his leering gaze back on me.

"We're playing the game by giving Lane Enterprises the Power Chip contract, but we'll be looking for other partnerships to better align with our ... interests moving forward."

It was pitiful really, how grown men seemed to think by dangling a carrot or a stick they could browbeat someone into submission. As if the shriveled carrot or the gnarled stick had any authority over me.

I brought my shark to the surface of my skin, allowing the steely determination of a predator to leach into my tone.

"You seem to think that I'm desperate to be at the top. I'm not. I have power because people want to give it to me. I have alliances because people know that they're betting on a sure thing."

I licked my lips and pasted on my most condescending smile, no longer in the mood to play a game of pretense.

Marco Alvarez had the audacity to believe he was invincible. I had removed the cocks of many an invincible man, and he was next in line.

"I was crowned Queen, Marco. I didn't need to take the throne to prove my dick is bigger than yours."

I slid out of my seat and smoothed down my skirt.

"No need to threaten me," I declared cheerfully. "I know exactly where I stand."

My face was frozen in its perfunctory mask, but I couldn't stop the challenging wink.

"I'll see you at the ribbon cutting on Friday."

And soon, I'll see you at my black site.

Cora Flynn

CHAPTER 15

Aaron

"You have a beautiful smile, Aaron. Please use it."

Hillary turned to face the cameras with a well-placed smile of her own as she muttered the admonishment under her breath; the quiet command hung loosely on her tongue.

I forced the subtle smile I had perfected in a mirror decades ago; one that conveyed warmth without attachment, humility without admission, charm without interest. A slight flash of teeth with a bow of my head. It would be all this crowd would get out of me today.

Not that I didn't agree with the cause. Our joint venture in the tech sphere would bring thousands of much-needed jobs into Carlisle and the surrounding towns. The educated and the blue-collar workers would get their equal share, and our company would reap the rewards of high profit in a boom market.

Money my parents had no rights to. Another move in the forward direction.

Hillary cut the garish pink ribbon that had been of her choosing with flourish, and the burgeoning crowd cheered when she tipped her glaring pink hardhat in their direction.

She was a beautiful showman, and the people loved her.

I was her accessory, the wealthy man she had convinced to be a part of the endeavor. The people couldn't care less about me, save for the cohort of women who continued to throw themselves at my feet, as if I would hand-select one of them to bring them to bed.

I squinted into the barrage of women who'd showed up today, all hovering at the front of the crowd like a pack of fertile wolves in stiletto heels and revealing skirts. I felt no emotion or desire whenever I briefly caught sight of their perky breasts and bright lips. Their bodies blurred together into one thirsty entity.

Surprise filled me when a familiar face held my stare in earnest—my employee from Club 7—the one whose name I didn't know.

A question from a media hack pulled my attention, and when I returned for a second glimpse, she was gone. But I was certain it had been her.

Why would a highly paid prostitute attend an event like this?

An irrelevant question when my life hung in the balance. Even so, it intrigued me. Perhaps I was clinging to any morsel of distraction that could relieve me of my mental burdens.

Hillary's soft hand landed gently in the small of my back and nudged me leftward to leave the podium. I cast one more practiced smile, waved to the crowd, and sauntered off into the wings of the makeshift public relations staging.

"What's with you today?" my blonde companion asked with a confused frown, her blue eyes scanning my face for any signs of inner turmoil. She was astute, *Mi Reina*, and she would read the story on my skin too clearly for comfort. I needed to divert her.

"You are not fucking me anymore," I commented casually, lazily rolling my neck and adjusting the cuffs on my suit jacket. "I'm finding it hard not to be … distracted."

It was not a lie, and yet, a total misdirection. I had missed the softness of her flesh and the warm slickness of her cunt, but I knew those days would come again—they always did. My conversation with Veronica and Vicente had left the rancid flavor of death on my tongue, and I had found no substance that would rid me of its sourness.

The breathy sound of an exasperated scoff met my ears. "Nice try. You have an entire arsenal of employees to help you with that problem. Tell me the truth."

Fire licked up my spine as I stared into her gaze, finding the fierce raging sea of challenge in her eyes. My redirect had been meant as her distraction, not mine, but I was finding them to be one and the same.

The corridor of the building was empty as the crowd dispersed beyond its walls. The factory would open tomorrow and welcome six hundred new employees to build computer parts for Google and Apple. But in this moment, we were alone.

I shifted my weight forward, closing in on her smaller frame like a predator cornering prey. She backed up against the wall, and allowed me to hover over her as I took up all the space between us.

I brought my face to hers and tilted my head to brush the bridge of my nose up the column of her neck, inhaling the notes of vanilla and honey in her perfume. She shuddered but made no move to lean into me. Instead, she tilted her head to the side, increasing my access to nip and suck at her pulse points.

"The truth, *Mi Reina*," I whispered into the shelter of her skin, "is when I am fucking them, I am fucking you. I only see your face. I only feel your wet cunt wrapped around me. I only feel your tight ass holding onto my cock." I wrapped my hand around hers and brought it to the swell of said cock in my dress pants, its angry head desperate for her touch. "If I need to vacate Club 7 to indulge in the real thing, so be it."

I ground my erection into her hand to further my point, then promptly released her and stepped away from the wall to allow us both a moment to cool down.

Her words from our previous encounter had stayed with me, despite my drunken haze. With Veronica and Vicente throwing me to my death, I would choose who to spend the remainder of my days with. It wasn't a choice at all–it was a compulsion, a reckoning.

The dazed clouds of her expression dissipated quickly, leaving a neutral mask behind.

"That's not what I meant, Aaron." She pushed off the wall and straightened her skirt, pulling the collar of her blouse up to hide the red patch of flesh I'd left in my wake. "I also never agreed to an exclusivity clause."

I quirked an amused brow. "Oh? I was under the impression Kellan was no longer a contender."

"Who said anything about Kellan?"

"You forget, *Mi Reina*—I have known you most of your life. You have a particularly fiery disposition when Kellan pisses you off. He has pissed you off, yes?"

Her glare was telling enough. "There is no exclusivity clause, Aaron."

I shrugged with indifference, unafraid of another man's position. I was not so filled with hubris to think I had any guarantee of living past my conversation with Antonio. I would take what I was offered in the time I had left.

"Attend the gala with me. We can discuss our reparations then." My phone buzzed in my pocket, and I took it out to skim the message. I frowned in irritation at the simple words on the screen.

"I have a prior commitment," she blurted, but didn't elaborate. "I'll meet you there—and then we can discuss … reparations."

"That is all I ask." I forced a smile and brushed a kiss against her cheekbone before heading down the hallway to prepare for my next meeting. The heaviness in my stomach for what I was about to do rose to the confines of my throat.

"I will see you soon," I promised, knowing full well that promise might not be kept.

"What is this about, Rodriguez?"

Kellan's gruff, booming voice was an irritant to my soul, grating my eardrums with the pompous command in his tone.

He exuded the arrogance of a man used to getting his own way, without the time or willingness to bend to the whims of others. My temperament was the same.

His presence held a power within it, quiet and controlled like a lion knowing nothing in the savanna could harm him save for another lion.

I was the other lion.

We were cut from the same cloth; whereas mine had been sewn into a fine suit, Kellan wore his like a caveman's cloak. Refined versus rugged. My smooth grace versus his rough saunter.

We stood in my newly acquired warehouse, now well into the construction stages. The powdery dust of freshly screwed drywall settled onto my skin in a fine mist and the fading scent of sawdust lingered in the cooling air of the evening. My teams were on track to meet my impossible timelines to get the building operational.

I had originally purchased the building as a way to secure the Rodriguez assets in this part of town; a stronghold for our legions of men to house our most valuable illegal assets in a secure facility on neutral ground.

All that had changed course with my parents' decision to join with the enemy they used to plot against. It was no longer a fortress against Alvarez as the Rodriguez heir, and I was going to have to decide what to do with a fortified climate-controlled, sound-proofed building with three bank vaults, a private fight ring with theater seating, and a dungeon-style fetish sex club. I had an idea, but it would only be useful if Antonio agreed.

Dead men couldn't run businesses—legal or otherwise.

"I have a proposition for you." I leaned against an abandoned ladder in the center of the room and folded my arms across my chest, grimacing at the layer of white chalk that had wiped off on my shirtsleeve.

"So?" Kellan mimicked my stance and tossed me a pointed glare. "Out with it."

"My parents are pulling out of the agreement. They've partnered with Alejandro Alvarez and have sent me to deliver the message. They are hoping you will kill me as penance, so they will be set free to carry out their whims as they see fit."

Kellan's bushy eyebrows raised a fraction. He brought his hand to his face and stroked down his short beard as his icy blue eyes stared through me. A jarring laugh burst from between his teeth, all but shattering my composure.

"You have big balls for a robot, Rodriguez. I'll give you that."

My lip curled into a sneer. "My *cajones* are not the topic of conversation. This is the position I have been put in. So, I have a counteroffer for you."

"Oh?"

"Give me their territory. I will operate against them and their alliance with Alvarez. This building is under construction to house much of our operations under one roof. Let my parents wallow in their misery with their poor choices when Antonio doles out punishment. I can be your ally."

I stood to my full height, dusted off my dirty sleeves, and faced him as the man I was; the equal lion. His face betrayed no emotion, but he shrewdly assessed my mask as if I was capable of letting my feelings slip through, unlike the robot he claimed me to be.

Bastard.

"You say a lot of pretty words, *Cabron*." He stepped forward, stopping a few feet in front of me. I refused to move. His next words would release me or seal me to my fate.

"You realize that this isn't up to me, right? Antonio wants to increase his cut, not lose it. He'll probably tell me to kill your parents, and then kill you for good measure. He's done worse for less—and you know this, or you wouldn't be coming to me."

I dipped my head, acknowledging that was true. Kellan might spare me, but Antonio surely wouldn't, not without someone arguing for my case.

A better man might attempt to leave this life—sell my shares and start new companies, or keep my shares and silently slink away to another end of the earth, away from the criminal empire I was blooded into.

I was not meant for picket fences and puppies. I was bred to build underground kingdoms of power and pain. I would leave in a body bag, but not sooner.

I had many men who were paid to die for me, but to what end? I did not want Antonio's position or that of Alvarez, ruling from a throne built on a pile of corpses. I was satisfied with my one kingdom, providing small, dark joys to the wayward masses in need of an escape. I did not need the promise of more.

"I am not so filled with pride I can't bargain for my life. If I am to be thrown to wolves, I can at least choose my pack, yes?"

The blond commander whistled through his teeth and shook his head, a meaty palm rubbing down his face. The tattoos along his knuckles taunted me—"hell" and "hope"— their jagged typeface a brutal reminder of the situation I found myself in.

"Alright. I'll take it to him, but you might not like the answer."

I nodded swiftly. "I will take that risk. When you have your answer, I will invite you back to show you what I have here. We could be good partners, you and I."

The grunt I received in return was not at all reassuring. I certainly didn't *want* to work with a man whose ego rivaled mine, but if that was what fate delivered, I would accept it.

It was better than a battle to the death. One I would not win.

He turned on his heel, footsteps echoing into the emptiness of the unfinished space as he left me and my destiny behind.

CHAPTER 16

Hillary

"Over here, Ms. Lane."

A balding man with watery eyes dressed in an impeccably pressed tuxedo led me into the ballroom of the Waldorf Estate. The grand room was bathed in the warm glow of gold paint, delicate crystals, and ancient tapestries of long-lost empires that cost as much as a small country's annual GDP.

Jediah Waldorf was the wealthiest man in the state, his inheritance and subsequent hotel empire rivaling mine. The entire home was lined with opulence and laced with exorbitance, but none of the tawdry exhibitions on display here tonight were likely to impress me.

The historic building held all sorts of treasures, but despite its familiarity, I detested the place. My childhood memories of coming here were cold, unfeeling ventures in dodging men with wandering eyes and boys with wandering hands.

Being born into the world as a blonde, blue-eyed little girl with an eventual Barbie figure had made me the enticing target of unwanted affections. Daddy didn't pay them much attention, but I had mastered my death stare long before I hit puberty, which usually kept the wolves at bay.

Until I became the wolf. It only took baring my teeth one time for all suggestive behavior to stop entirely.

Well, teeth, a well-aimed knee to the scrotum, and a forceful punch to the solar plexus. It was my first real-world Krav Maga experience, though I wouldn't start my actual training until years later.

One moment in your life can change the entire course of your existence. When I fought back, and fought back hard, I'd set a limit and sent a message. So much so, I'd tricked myself into a false sense of security—I conned myself into believing I could protect everyone around me too.

It was the hardest lesson I'd ever learned. A mistake I was still trying to atone for. I shook the suffocating thoughts aside. Now wasn't the time to be brooding about the past.

My eyes scanned the room, assessing the growing number of guests in their formal wear. My gaze caught on the unmistakably muscled form of a large man in a deep blue, perfectly tailored pinstriped suit. Even from a fifty-foot distance, Kellan could take a woman's breath away.

His hair was down this evening, landing just below his shoulder blades. The windswept style framed his high cheekbones and brought out the reddish undertones in the stubble that smoothed out his firm jaw. He was speaking to a woman I didn't recognize; a stunning brunette dressed in a revealing emerald gown, their heads bowed together like they were sharing a delicious secret.

Of course, I should have expected he'd be here. Only a few privileged people knew about Kellan's dual alliances; anyone in this crowd would know him as a key player in a powerful network of black-market businesses, not as an equally powerful member of the Federal Bureau of Investigation.

I tamped down the uncomfortable feeling of jealousy masking as annoyance and turned around to scope out the other end of the vast luxurious space.

Surprise immediately replaced my irritation. Jonah and Mical Carlos, Kellan's twin brothers, and the current operators of the Carlos Cartel in our region, sat stone-faced as usual at a nearby table. An animated, attractive Latino man was attempting to engage them in conversation, but getting not even a single murmur of response.

I snorted. I had experienced the twins at their most charming at past dinners. Like Kellan, they were highly trained, lethal soldiers; dangerous men in pretty packaging. Unlike Kellan, they were more than willing to carry out Big Bad Daddy's orders without question or context, and had a vicious trail of bodies in their wake to prove it.

I generally steered clear of them. I had no idea why they'd be here this evening when Kellan was already here to represent 'the family', but Antonio Carlos and his merry band of illegitimate sons weren't my problem to solve or my crusade to carry; I had larger dicks to chop off in this town. Had Daddy not been best friends with a dead Carlos son, I might never have gotten involved with Kellan in the first place.

Some days, I wished I never had.

"Ms. Lane?"

The geriatric guide looked at me expectantly. He pointed a gnarled finger at the empty seat in front of him. My name was written in elegant script at the place setting.

"Yes, thank you." I nodded brusquely and placed my clutch against the bone China dishware, effectively dismissing my escort.

"*Mi Reina.*"

The familiar, soothing scent of sandalwood and vanilla blanketed me from behind; Aaron.

Large hands skated up my bare arms and spun me around, pulling me toward him for a light, perfunctory hug.

In a crowded room filled with career criminals, I could lean into his touch without repercussion. I could caress him like a lover; no one would bat an eye. The depraved part of me wanted to mark him in the middle of the crowd; claim him.

I pulled back and took in the man. The crisp gray suit molded to every peak and valley of his body, highlighting developed shoulders and a narrow waist. His hair was loose and combed to one side and the dark natural waves framed his cheekbones. Captivating brown eyes peered back at me, twinkling with muted amusement.

"Have you forgiven me, *Mi Reina*? Or am I still on your chopping block?"

"Another unfortunate soul has taken that position." I quipped, working hard to keep the smile off my lips. "You're relieved for today."

A rare, heart-faltering grin took over the brooding businessman's face. "I pity that man."

He moved to pull my chair out from the table, gesturing for me to sit.

"You don't want to speak to these people, anyway." He nodded to the crowd swelling on all sides. "Come, we have business to discuss."

I frowned, but took the seat anyway as the Rodriguez heir settled in beside me. He angled his body to face mine, leaning in like we were sharing secrets.

"My parents and I are at an impasse," he murmured while his fingers discreetly caressed the soft skin of my shoulder. "I am working out the particulars on my end, but they are shifting alliances."

He reached for my chin, using his thumb and forefinger to tilt my head to meet his eyes. Warm, honest eyes.

"I have given you my loyalty, *Reina*. Trust whatever it is I have nothing to do with it."

It was rare to see Aaron let his guard down like this, to allow me to see directly into his soul, whatever remained of it. He was usually clinical in these kinds of crowds. Incredibly charming when the cause suited, but mostly aloof, unattached to life in ways that most of us were.

He had called me his 'queen' since we were fourteen, but only ever in private. My arranged marriage had been a poorly guarded secret, so through our childhoods, we'd been nothing more than familiar teenagers at our parents' parties, playing our parts as dutiful heirs.

The first time I had sex with him, I'd just returned home from college desperate for a release and to escape my haunted memories. We played our perfunctory roles for the better part of the evening, but what I remembered most was he'd been happy–a gold spark in his eye that rarely took hold, and it had changed his entire appeal.

I'd kissed him in the limo we'd opted to share to get us home; he kissed me back without a fraction of hesitation, and we didn't make it out of the car before abandoning our clothes and fucking like we were the last two people on earth.

Whether it was the years of brothel management or a natural affinity, Aaron was amazing in bed.

Somehow, over the years, we'd remained that way. Never together, but somehow, never truly apart.

Now looking into the unfiltered truth in deep pooling brown, I believed him. If Aaron was telling me anything at all about his parents' dealings, it was a move in the right direction, for *our* partnership. *Our* future.

I had received the completed paperwork earlier that afternoon. Despite the public protests and familial interference, all of our previously agreed-to terms were signed off. It would have given me a catty sense of satisfaction, but the entire delay had unnecessarily put a wedge between us. With so few friends in this world, I didn't want another enemy.

So, I hadn't lied. Aaron was currently off my shit list. But it was an ever-changing list and today's version had no bearing on tomorrow's status.

He'd do well to remember it.

"Hillary!"

Jediah's simpering tenor snapped me out of the conversation before I could even acknowledge the reparation. His ingratiating voice injected steel into my spine and I drew in a breath so that I too could spew the same bullshit.

"Jediah!" I plastered on my most seasoned smile and stood to give the five-foot-six man a stilted hug. "What a wonderful turnout this evening."

A conceited sneer rivaling the Cheshire Cat smiled back at me, and I stifled the urge to smack it off his face.

"So lovely to see you again, darling." He turned to face Aaron, who had moved to stand beside me in silent partnership. "So good to see you, son. I look forward to sharing your family's announcement later this evening. The power players—they are shifting! And ah!"

The giddy host spotted someone behind us and waved them over. "There is someone I'd like you to meet."

I didn't shift my stance to see who it was. Anyone I needed or wanted to know at these particular gatherings, I had already met. Aaron and I exchanged a look of mutual distaste for another introduction, but I prepared my most saccharine smile to get the encounter over with.

"Oy', Jed!"

The resonance of the Irish lilt was unmistakable. Lauchlan O'Donnell, in the very flesh, had received an invite to an elite, private gathering of the wealthy from Jediah Waldorf himself.

Tasty thoughts of the debauchery in my living room the other night rose to the surface, and I could feel my core heating from the memories. Nothing got me off more than the ability to incapacitate a man through his own pleasure. By his submission or my servitude was irrelevant; through either mechanism, I was the one in full control. I relished it.

The way he had taken ownership of my control, how deeply he'd leaned into it ... I tamped the feelings down as quickly as they had come. Lauchlan was a new sort of control for me now.

He appeared a second later, and I assessed him under a new lens with my latest information. His unruly auburn hair was combed away from his face and the stubble across his cheeks and chin had been finely trimmed into a roguish shadow. His muscular body fit his light blue suit nicely, bringing out the deeper greens and flecks of gold in his eyes.

Even at a quick glance, he had the natural ability to stand out from the crowd, but also blended in seamlessly, as if you'd only noticed him because he wanted you to. He held himself casually, non-threateningly, with a detached confidence that appeared safe.

All masterful traits for swindling the masses.

Pouty lips broke out into a cheeky grin as he likely assumed I was checking him out instead of eyeing up an opponent.

Just you wait, my little rook.

"Have you met Lauchlan? He's new in town, but comes from a very established Galway family. I'm sure he'll be making a name for himself here in no time."

Lauchlan took my hand with a flourish and discreetly stroked the underside of my palm with his thumb. The subtle gesture sprouted more tingling in my belly. Another tamp down.

I dropped his hand and smiled surreptitiously. "We've met, yes."

The Irish swindler's sea-glass eyes flared with heat before a swift blink wiped all desire away. A quick wink and flash of perfect teeth followed, veiling his interest as mostly professional.

I'd never pegged a business associate to seal a deal, but we could certainly keep up appearances.

Aaron draped a casual arm around my back and I stifled a bark of laughter at the obvious territorial move. All the money and intellect in the world, and the man was, at his core, still a Neanderthal.

I gently pulled away from his grasp and beckoned for Lauchlan to sit across the table from us.

"Take a seat." I echoed the words from our previous night in a dramatically different context. The charming con artist didn't miss the reference and grinned impishly, batting the name card of an 'Ira Robinson' off of his chosen place setting before he unbuttoned his suit jacket to settle in at our table.

Aaron shot me a begrudging look, the muscle of his sharp, stubbled jaw pulsing in irritation as he pulled out my seat again, taking his place beside me with a huff.

Jediah clapped his hands together, gold bracelets on both wrists rattling in time to his movements. "Wonderful! I'll leave you to it."

The garish man trotted away, spying another unwitting victim among the masses.

My gaze trailed after him, curious what he was up to. Our opportunistic host wasn't 'introducing' Lauchlan to us as a point of practiced pleasantries. Why was he placing an apparently skilled career criminal in our sights? Successful criminals built their reputations through a well-honed network—was Jediah one of his contacts?

If he was, Lauchlan had more roots on American soil than I originally thought.

I turned my attention back to the men at my table. The silent pissing contest between a set of dancing green eyes and glowering brown ones filled the air with the thick fog of testosterone and stupidity.

My perfectly polished smile held in place while I inwardly cackled at the fun this night was turning out to be. Jediah's parties were normally a predictable snooze of well-timed barbs and the trading of illicit information—snooze fests I needed to attend to keep a pulse on the ever-changing landscape of power. This palpable masculine tension was a scream in comparison.

"How did you two meet?"

Aaron's authoritative tenor crackled in the air between us, and I offered him nothing but a coy smile.

"Do you remember the friend I mentioned when I ran into you at Quintessence? The meeting you 'forgot' to invite me to?" I dipped my head toward Lauchlan's beaming smirk as he took a sip of wine from the crystal goblet set in front of him. "Lucky and I were just having a drink. Getting to know each other." I shrugged dismissively. "I discovered he doesn't like choking nearly as much as some men."

The smirk transformed into choked coughs as wine sprayed from Lauchlan's lips to cover the plate in front of him.

My flippant taunts weren't meant to wound—they had just enough bite to cause a mild sting; a sting Aaron could more than handle, and dish out, on a good day. Today, his glowering blossomed into a sanctimonious sneer, the perfect replica of his father.

"Perhaps he has never been properly choked."

The energy of one of the most powerful men on this side of the country rolled off him in waves as he stared through the still smirking Irishman as if his eyes could set him on fire. "I'll give you a pass to my club, my friend. My employees will attend to your most interesting proclivities."

Lauchlan's smile was innocent, but his eyes held a wickedness I would one day use against him.

"No need, mate. I've found the perfect person to satisfy my"—he moved his fingers into air quotes and raised the pitch of his voice in a mocking tone—"'proclivities'. But I hope you get a real good choking some day soon, yeah? Might loosen that stick out of your arse—"

"Lauchlan," I interrupted coolly before Aaron could grind his teeth into a curb. "I never caught what you do for a living?"

Glossy green eyes turned their gaze back to me, and I just caught the glimpse of the roiling depths within them before they shuttered back to their brilliant hue.

"Tech, love. I'm in tech."

Smoothly delivered, vague, and uninteresting. How practiced.

"I've never fully understood what that means." I turned to the simmering man beside me and gently squeezed his bicep. "Have you, Aaron? Do you know what being 'in tech' means?"

The chestnut lashes of the Columbian man's eyes rose with darkly amused interest as I cut through the tension radiating from his core. "At the risk of sounding ignorant, I do not know what"—he mimed his own air quotes mockingly—"'being in tech' means."

Kellan's ill-timed interruption saved the suave Irishman with his rehearsed lines.

The Viking had finally found me—his piercing blue gaze locked onto mine like a missile and his massive form lumbered toward our table.

"Hillary." He nodded curtly to Aaron, his gaze not breaking from mine for a second. "Rodriguez."

Lauchlan stood and held a hand out to Kellan. "Lauchlan O'Donnell, mate. Heard lots of rumors about the big baddies on this side of the pond. Looking forward to getting acquainted."

Kellan finally broke our silent staring contest to turn toward our cheeky guest, his limbs visibly freezing on the spot as he took Lauchlan in. His icy stare squinted—the barest hint of recognition flashing before he adopted the signature neutral mask of the true cartel leader he was.

"I don't shake hands." He positioned his body away from Lauchlan by taking the other seat on my left, boxing me between him and Aaron.

"Don't do a lot of things, ay?"

There it was again—the smallest flicker of acknowledgment across Kellan's features. Well, wasn't this a tasty nugget of information? Was I Lauchlan's only target, or was he casing our fair little town of the rich and famous?

If he was reckless enough to swindle Antonio's sons, he was far more dangerous than I realized. I'd get Blackbird to up her surveillance.

I turned my attention back to the moody King of Iceland.

"How nice to see you." I kept my tone level, folding my arms across my chest. "Does this mean your tantrum is over, or will I wait another six months like the last time?"

Aaron didn't bother to muffle his snort; Lauchlan's lips twitched into an amused smirk. The searing singe from Kellan's glare may have burned a lesser person—but it barely tickled my funny bone.

Before he could bite out a snarky retort, the abrupt clang of a ceremonious gong sounded from a small platform built at the front of the large room, signaling the standing guests to take their seats.

"Thank you all for coming this evening." Veronica Rodriguez's smooth Spanish accent washed over the audience as she took her position at the podium on the platform.

The stunning woman reminded me of Sofia Vergara; she too was Columbian, with a temperate grace and the body of a supermodel. Whereas Sofia seemed very genuine and sweet in all of her interviews, Veronica was oleander in human form; beautiful to look at, deadly poison to touch.

I had touched her once, back when I believed pretty things had pretty souls. Some of our most valuable lessons were the hardest to learn.

The toxic woman surveyed the crowd with a serene smile and continued. "I am pleased to be here with Vicente, and I'd like to thank Jediah for hosting us in his beautiful home once again."

Polite applause broke out around us. Aaron stiffened beside me, his taut body vibrating with anticipation. I slid my hand onto his thigh under the table and squeezed his molded quad in solidarity.

Whatever our differences and whatever our future, I couldn't let him face a family betrayal alone. I knew how deep that wound would run, how cancerous that tissue was.

"Before we get started, Vicente and I have some news to share with you before we go public to the world tomorrow."

"Rodriguez Industries is taking a fresh course into the future. Our son, Aaron, has taken our subsidiary in a different direction—one we wish him well on, but want no part in. Tomorrow, Rodriguez Industries will be united with our largest South American competitor, Predrolas. We are thrilled to partner with Alejandro Alvarez and his sons."

A low murmur rippled through the tables around us as she carried on.

"This acquisition will make us the highest valued company in the state, the fourth largest in America. We hope you'll continue to work with us on our many … endeavors."

Even from this distance, I could sense the knowing glint in her eye, as she'd just subtly invited the morally gray crowd to continue to support their underground activities.

This acquisition would rival the size of Aaron's and my new company, but that was hardly something I cared about. I didn't need to be the 'best', the 'biggest'—that was for egotistical men who constantly needed to measure their dick to justify their own existence. We were very good at what we did and would continue to be so, Veronica and her simpering pomp aside.

But Alejandro Alvarez … 'coincidence' was a word people used to tidily package up things they didn't understand. I didn't believe in coincidences.

Jediah had taken the podium now, but the men seated around my table snared my attention.

Lauchlan—not his real name—O'Donnell, the con-artist heir who was, in theory, attempting to swindle me out of my fortune, looked more curious than conflicted as he watched the buzzing crowd with interest.

Kellan Carlos, the heir to the Cartel throne and FBI crusader. His ticking jaw and wrathful scowl looked like he could crack a skull at the recent announcement. I didn't need to know all the ins and outs of the Carlos Cartel empire to know this move would give Alvarez an advantage in taking over territory.

Aaron Rodriguez, the billionaire heir to a family company who dabbled in the dirty, depraved side of the rich and famous, had been ousted by his parents in a public display of denouncement—because of the choices he made with me.

And me—heiress, mogul, and self-appointed vigilante, who would protect innocent girls and women at *any* cost. Which meant I now had a *very* vested interest in Alejandro Alvarez.

I blew out a breath, then inhaled a renewed sense of purpose for the days ahead.

I would figure out what Kellan was hiding from me.

I would make Lauchlan regret his decision to target me.

I would dig into the debauched deeds of the Rodriguez family and expose them as the sex-trafficking scum of the earth they were. In my heart, I had to believe Aaron wasn't a part of it, but if he was ... well, my vengeance spared no one.

It was a good thing gray was my color, because we were about to be wearing a whole lot of it.

CHAPTER 17

Kellan

"**F**or *once* in your life, Kellan. Can you be less of an ass?"

I folded my paper down in front of me, unsurprised to see Hillary's feisty expression. She was earlier than I'd expected, but I knew she'd be showing up at some point after Jediah's farce of a party the other night.

She couldn't resist the opportunity for a fight, especially with me.

"How nice to see you," I intoned passively, setting aside the newspaper and folding my arms across my chest. "Please, come in."

How she had found me here, in the stark, pseudo-FBI office in the nondescript building ten blocks from her condo, wasn't a question. She'd been keeping tabs on me for years, just as I had her.

She was too much of a firecracker, too ballsy, to walk right into a dangerous situation, and just competent enough to get herself out. She was the worst kind of person to care about from afar, but over the last six years I'd done my best, even if my best had let her little vigilante crusade go unnoticed before she'd done significant damage.

Cutting off cocks. I bit the inside of my cheek to keep the smirk off my face as she glared daggers at me in a pink power suit. Of course, that would be her chosen punishment. The tiny blonde castrater was every man's worst nightmare, and most men's wet dream.

She haunted both of mine; the savage need to keep her safe and the selfish desire to keep her away from this life I'd built were always at war—asleep and awake.

"To what do I owe the pleasure, Killer?"

We continued our stare down, not giving the other an inch. It was always like this with her; the push and pull of a rubber band close to snapping.

"Tell me why the fuck, two days after the Rodriguez' announce their little 'departure', I'm being investigated for workplace harassment?"

I squinted at the piece of paper crumpled within her fist. Wordlessly, I held out a hand. She all but threw it into my face.

I smoothed out the official-looking court document on the surface of my desk and scanned through it. It was a fake —a solid forgery—but definitely fake.

"This isn't ours, Hill. Somebody is fucking with you."

She sputtered and for a split-second, she had nothing to say. That reprieve didn't last long, though.

"This isn't yours?"

She leveled those sky-blue eyes at me, not wanting to believe me, but clearly not wanting the opposite, either.

I matched her stare, leaning in to the depthless eyes where I loved to fall when she gave me total control. It had been too long, but not nearly long enough. I put on the brakes every time I started to crave her, knowing my sobriety did nothing to solve my addiction to her smell, her skin, her taste.

"No." It was a simple answer. There was no investigation, not by this division, but someone did a decent enough job to make the doc look real.

A haughty blonde brow raised in annoyance.

"Then help me catch the fucker who's wasting my time," she snapped, but the demand had less bite than her original entrance.

She folded herself into the twenty-dollar office chair and kicked off her heels, stretching her body out with the grace of a panther. I knew just how lithe that body could be, on the mat and in my bed.

"Is this sort of 'help' the same as your version of Guantanamo?" I stood from my cheap seat in need of a stretch myself and ambled to the front of the desk. Leaning against it, I stared down my nose at her. Like it or not, she would get this message. "I'm not helping you with any more of that shit, Killer."

"You secured me a small piece of real estate, Kellan," she retorted, meeting my stare with a fiery one of her own. "How typical of a man to make himself more important than he is."

I didn't stifle the snort this time. "Cute." I picked up the wrinkled paper and held it up to the light. "I'm going to keep this, but the FBI isn't interested in you. *You're* not that important."

If the FBI knew exactly what she was up to in the late hours with Sammy and her crack team, they would very much be interested, but I'd covered up any trace of what she hadn't already done herself.

I would make sure they—we—never found her, even if she was cutting off cocks.

A condescending, unamused scoff escaped those pillowy lips, but she was undeterred, as always. I loved her fierceness. Even if it made me want to smother her with a pillow on a good day.

"What do you know about Alvarez, Kellan?"

She switched gears faster than I expected, but I should have known the question was coming. Maybe she forged the document herself as a reason to barge in on me—nothing was off the table when Hillary was on a mission. But I was serious about this one. If Antonio and Alvarez were about to go head-to-head, this town—this state—was about to get a hell of a lot more dangerous.

I leaned over the rickety chair, surrounding her with my bulk and the heat of my body. The floral notes on her skin were as familiar as the smell of her cunt when she was desperate for me, and both brought the same reaction to the head of my dick.

I lowered my mouth to her ear, brushing my lips against the shell. "Listen carefully, my pretty little killer. A bigger game is being played here. I don't know all the players yet, but this town is on the verge of a turf war, and I'll chain you to a fucking wall myself if it means you're not getting in the middle of it."

She pushed at my chest, barely budging me, but her tone was acidic enough to burn. "I know how to dance with demons, Kellan. If Alvarez is bringing unwilling girls into this town, I'll kill him before he gets the chance to kill them."

Before now, I'd assumed this crusade was just another cause this woman liked to chase—something to validate the pure chance of being born into extreme wealth and needing to compensate for it. The vehemence in her tone was as familiar to me as if I'd said the words myself.

The truth was written in the clench of her jaw and the intense determination in her eyes. I'd been wrong. The castrations were personal. When something was personal, nothing would stop her from finishing what she'd started. Even if that goal was impossible, like keeping the flesh market out of the state. Antonio himself didn't have that kind of power.

Sick men and women would always take advantage of other men and women. It was a sad truth of life. Hillary would never achieve her goal.

She likely knew that. My killer was the smartest person in the room most times; she knew the statistics; she knew the risks. Acid bubbled to the base of my esophagus at what that meant.

Hillary had unresolved trauma with a sexual predator and was playing Batwoman to ease the burden. The acerbic taste burned a hole through my stomach; I'd need a full bottle of Tums later.

How had I not known this? And who would I have to kill to take it away from her?

Bitter resignation replaced the caustic burn and its gnawing teeth bit through the base of my ribcage and into my heart.

"What is it going to take to get you to stand down, Hill?" I lowered my guard for one brief second, giving her the smallest glimpse of my pain. "I can't protect you from him."

Whether I meant Alvarez or Antonio, it didn't matter. Hillary hid behind bold confidence and billions of dollars, but these men were far more ruthless. They weren't concerned about saving innocents—young girls or beautiful billionaires; if she was a problem, they would eliminate her.

Antonio would send *me* to eliminate her.

He was still pissed at her father for the trouble he'd caused the cartel years before, and didn't need another reason to look her way. It was why I'd put distance between us every time I felt her pull a bit too much. I was a weapon for my father, and nothing else. And if he knew the truth about how I felt about her?

He'd use her as a weapon against me.

"Kell—I don't need your protection." Hillary worried her lip between her teeth. The rare uncertainty made my chest twinge. "I need your *help*."

Raw irritation filled her features moments before her brows molded into a hesitant frown.

I blew out a breath. Hillary Lane never asked for help. She demanded it, she threatened for it, but she'd never *asked* me for anything before now; this time, we were partners instead of opposing forces.

Her blue eyes blazed, but they were rimmed with forlorn pain.

"I've had to clean up three more hitters in the last month. All well-known men, all girls supplied by Alvarez. One was as young as fifteen."

Her voice faltered, barely noticeable, but it held the resignation of someone who blamed themselves.

"I can't keep chasing him from behind, Kell. I can't keep walking in at the very last second before these people are destroyed. Sometimes"—she drew in a sharp breath, as if the words themselves brought on too much pain —"sometimes, I'm too late."

Before I could stop myself, I pulled her the few inches into my arms and wrapped my biceps tightly around her shoulders. She didn't lean into me for a solid few seconds before giving up on being stubborn and settling into my comfort.

I'd held her like this before, but only ever after sex. Never as a simple offer of support. It wouldn't be the first time I wished I could be this man for her. But I'd long since let go of that fantasy—choosing instead to take what I could get.

"You can't keep doing this, Killer," I murmured into the top of her head. "Period," She started to pull away. "I'll help you, but it's going to have to be on my terms. Otherwise, we're both dead."

She slipped out of my grasp, and her mask of cool neutrality was firmly back in place. "I'll consider it." Even her voice didn't shake.

I stood out of my crouched position and stepped back, giving her space to move out of the seat. She straightened her skirt and combed a few idle fingers through her hair, refusing to make eye contact. Then she flashed me a terse smile.

"We'll talk soon." Her tone made us sound like professional acquaintances instead of the complicated lovers we were. I hated that tone—but I had no one to blame but myself.

I nodded once and leaned back against the desk to watch her walk down the narrow hall to the stairs.

I didn't know how the fuck this was going to work, but I'd have to think of something. Fast.

Otherwise, my killer was going to be the one who got killed.

An insidious sense of unease burned a hole through my guts as I drove through the quiet streets of a small suburb to my makeshift 'home' whenever I was in Carlisle.

The bungalow wasn't modern or flashy like the condo in California, or rustic like my cabin in the Nevada mountains, but it was the least likely place anyone would expect me to live, so it was the first place I bought years ago.

Not that I was there much. A few weeks a year here and there, when I needed to check in on my brothers or oversee Cartel business. It was rare I was in town for FBI operations, and the international theft ring Trish had called me in to investigate was turning out to be more sophisticated than anticipated.

My team had uncovered a group called 'The Six'—a Board of Directors with a very complicated trail of bank accounts in Zurich and the Caymans who seemed to offer their services to the highest bidder.

My realm of criminal activity had nothing to do with high-value theft, but Jediah's did, and I'd taken the opportunity to pick his brain at his pretentious party the other night. The brunette he'd introduced me to was their 'connector' – the middle woman who vetted the client and the mark—now I was waiting for the lead to come through while my team continued to chase money trails on the other side of the world.

I'd pretend to want to stiff someone, hire them to do it, and steer the FBI right to the source. Then I could pack up my things and walk away from this shitty town.

If only. I could have said that yesterday, maybe, before I'd held Hillary in my arms and she'd asked for my help. I wouldn't leave her behind—not again.

I pulled into the average paved driveway with weeds growing up through the cracks. Turning off the car, I took a minute to sit in the dark before making the call.

"You're late."

Antonio answered in Spanish, his smooth tenor clipped in annoyance. At the tinkle of crystal through the line, I imagined him pouring a glass of his favorite exorbitant scotch. I hoped to poison it one day.

"Working on a case." I grunted, a subtle reminder I had other responsibilities—to his benefit—keeping me from being at his beck and call.

"And this case is more important than me?" His words were mocking, but his tone was flat.

"This case will throw the heat off our next set of problems," I countered and sank into the fabric chair of the sedan, closing my eyes. "The Rodriguezes have aligned themselves with Alvarez. Aaron came to me with the message."

The stillness on the other end was deceptively calm, but the sound of shattered glass came a second later.

"Aaron came to me," I amended, massaging my temples in anticipation of the inevitable headache, "and wants to work out a deal. He wasn't a part of the decision and will trade his life to work against them. He has some contingencies in place to make that happen."

Another pause.

"A man's loyalty to his family should never be questioned." Antonio's words were said with a finality I saw coming from a mile away. "If Aaron chooses to turn his back on his family, he will choose to turn his back on us."

I didn't care about Aaron Rodriguez one way or another—but he meant something to Hillary. She wouldn't forgive me if I was the one to put the bullet in his brain, but I wouldn't be able to protect her if I disobeyed a direct order.

I weighed my words carefully. "Perhaps his family has turned their back on him."

"A man who does not hold his parents' honor is not a man." Antonio's response brooked no arguments. "Kill him to send a message and frame Alvarez for the crime. Two birds with one stone."

The directive sealed Aaron's fate; there wasn't a damn thing I could do about it.

"As you wish."

My father continued, the sentencing a man to death for someone else's choices of no further concern. We all held the

Carlos callousness close to our hearts, but Antonio's was particularly pure.

"Assemble your brothers. We will start cleaning out the filth of Alvarez and his company."

I hung up the call and scrubbed my palms across my face. Blocking out all emotion, I considered the task ahead of me. It was just another nail in my coffin—when I finally met my end, there was no place for me but the bowels of hell.

It was only a matter of time before I joined Aaron there.

CHAPTER 18

Lauchlan

"Oy, Conan."

I slid onto the weight bench right next to the barbarian as he tried his best to bust a bicep with the weight he was pressing.

I barely got a head turn from the sexy oaf, all sputtering and sweating like a Canadian lumberjack. If I didn't already know how the fucker felt through my arse cheeks, I'd be tempted to give it a go in the shower again before he headed off to behead people, or whatever it was mobsters did after the gym.

"Little birdie told me you made a 'special request'"—I took out my best obnoxious air quotes—"to have my membership dismissed."

The Viking still wouldn't make eye contact, but I caught him sneak a little peek at me through the mirrors ahead. I stared into the reflection of that icy blue eye of his, not able to contain my grin.

"Couldn't imagine why you wouldn't want to work out with your cock-cozy," I announced with mock indignance, raising my voice with each word. "Aren't I a great cock-cozy, baby?"

The bar with all the weight of a small grizzly slammed back down and my buff target shot up from his seat, skin glistening and chest heaving—the sex appeal of this man really was top-notch. He glared at me like he hoped his eyes were laser beams and they'd cut me in half.

"Evidently, you have friends here." Kellan's voice was gravelly, unamused and unimpressed.

"That I do, my broody barbarian." Me and the Cheshire Cat had matching smiles this morning. "But don't you fret. We're going to be seeing a lot more of each other, mate."

I winked and hopped off the bench, taking in the angry, sculpted sight of him for one last blissful second. "I'll see you in the shower? If you"—obnoxious air quotes again, just for good measure—"'do that' anymore."

I chuckled all the way down the hallway to the cardio room, eager for a good run before I attempted to make good on my promise. Sweaty shower sex was the best sex if the cartel baddie would give me round two. A man could only hope.

He hadn't known who I was the last time I let him rail me in the gym shower. He still didn't, if Jediah's little criminal club party was any indication. I knew how to seduce a man as well as I could seduce any woman, and Kellan hadn't been hard pickings that day.

I could always tell when an Alpha male needed to let out a little frustration. They walked around like a Neanderthal, brows crunched together and bulky shoulders all tense and hard. Like they wanted to smash something. More like they needed to smash *someone*.

A little well-placed positioning, a few well-timed glances, and if there was interest, I could shag a shower mate in less than fifteen minutes.

It was hard to be me, really. It was a sacrifice to offer my body to men and women to be fondled and sucked and fucked dry. Someone throw me a right old pity party later.

Kellan wasn't a mark—not officially, at any rate—but I wanted him close. For my plan with Alvarez to work, I needed one of his kind in my back pocket. What could be closer than a man you let fuck you in a public loo?

He wasn't the type of man I could find on the fuck-n-chuck *Grinder*. I had scoped out his gym and got a membership. I bet on timing and chance and did a bit of research. If he hadn't been into men, I would have befriended ol' Kell-Bell and caught him in my net that way.

'Lucky' for me—I loved my new little nickname—he was *very* much into men. Or his dick was a sensational liar.

Two sexy projects I had on the go. If I had time before all the pieces were in play, I'd see what I could do to bring the three of us together.

I finished my workout and casually searched the bench area before heading back to the showers alone. I could have used another feisty shag today, but I'd made my point.

Kellan was clearly a Dom, and there was nothing a Dom enjoyed more than bringing a brat to their knees. I could be a brat to get his pants down; through that, I'd get his guard down too.

I'd take that pity party now.

Three weeks working for Alvarez was the typical snooze fest that came with working in tech. The team of software engineers and developers I managed were the stereotypical lot of socially awkward geniuses who'd spent all of ten minutes in a pub.

Hard to have them develop a hook-up app when I was sure most of them had never touched a real dickybird.

It wasn't a problem, really. I'd design the app in my sleep and give my crackpot team the credit. It was a simple premise and an easy interface. It just needed to be designed by someone who actually understood human behavior.

I was the man for that job.

I wasn't here to make Marco Alvarez another billion dollars. Quite the opposite, if I could get into the system I needed. That was the *real* job.

I stood from the cubicle in my team's 'bull pen'—Americans had some of the craziest names for things—and stretched my arms over my head, done with this façade of a day.

Marco offered me an office, but I didn't need some pretentious setup to make myself feel important on what was already a farce of a job.

I worked beside my team when I needed to show up at all, and pried as best I could in a group of people who didn't talk. It was incredible how thirty euros worth of pizza and a case of watery beer could open up a crowd better than any crock of 'team-bonding.'

"Gertie," I called out as walked down the hall toward her desk. "What do you say we go for dinner tonight?"

My cute little administrator giggled sheepishly. I'd learned she was quite the powerhouse of her own, knowing all the ins and outs of the Alvarez empire like nobody's business. She struggled with outright attention, so I lavished her with it, determined to bring that little blush to her cheeks every day.

"Mr. O'Donnell," she sputtered, to my amusement, "I told you I like women, right? I don't think I'm the kind of company you're looking for."

"Even better!" I chirped enthusiastically, flashing her a wide smile. "We can observe all the beautiful things in life together over tacos and go home with no expectations."

At her relieved smile, I shot off a cheeky wink. "I'm an excellent wingman, too, if something pretty catches your eye."

Another delightful sputter and cough. "I'll keep that in mind. I love tacos, though."

"Great!" I pulled her coat off the rack behind her desk and nodded toward her computer monitor, catching a quick glimpse of the files there. "We've both been here long enough." I held out her coat in offering. "Join me?"

Gertie's chagrin turned into a soft smile. "You're quite the charmer, you know that?"

She shut down her computer with the company passcode and I managed to get the first four digits of five. She shrugged on her coat as we walked down the stairs and out toward the street.

Our building was smack dab in the middle of downtown Carlisle. Ma's condo was only a few blocks from here, and Hillary's building was just down the street. I liked the proximity here—nothing like Dublin's streetscape.

We walked down to the Mexican restaurant at the other end of the row. Gertie chatted her little head off about growing up in Indiana and I filled in the space where I could. It was easy to let her talk—the more she talked, the more comfortable she'd be with telling me anything.

That, and I liked the sound of her pitchy Midwest accent. Gertie was cute as a button. I'd see what I could do to get her a nice girl to fuck tonight. I eyed up her sweet cheeks and wide eyes as I opened the door to the eatery—well, at least strike up a yarn with. Gertie didn't strike me as a fuck once kind of woman.

My mouth watered as the scent of grilled meats and spice hit us. We were brought to a table in the center of the room. Tacos were a street food where I came from, but apparently, in America, they also classified as fine dining.

No matter. Gertie deserved a good meal for putting up with the likes of a git like Marco, and I wasn't hard up for cash.

I'd have retired by the time I was twenty-five if I followed Da's advice and invested the take of my first few jobs. Thanks to his legacy, I'd started out when I was a lad, joining Da or Ma on scopes when they needed a kid to help their cover.

We once holidayed on the Italian coast as a family when I was nine—one particular job where they'd worked together for the better part of a month. I lounged with my nanny for most of it, but occasionally, I got to attend a yacht party with a bunch of rich saps while Ma and Da worked over the billionaire for a priceless piece of jewelry.

I was the one who'd sneaked the ring out while Ma improvised a distraction. It had been my first taste of the thrill of risk and reward, and I hadn't looked back. Even if I had the billions to my name like the likes of the Rodriguez empire or my tasty little project, I couldn't imagine a life doing anything but.

My master's degree in Software Engineering from King's College had been to suit my own interests, and I had to convince Da it wasn't a waste of time. I still ran jobs for The Six in London while I was there, which seemed to soothe his ire a titch. It was a useful cover more often than not.

So, while I wasn't flying anyone out on holiday in a private jet, I could well pay for my needs for the rest of my life, should I live that long.

Paying seventy dollars for a taco seemed a bit dodgy, though.

I looked up from my menu to see Gertie's eyes blinking rapidly, a hesitant frown on her cute-as-a-button face. Either she was allergic to tacos or was allergic to the prices.

"Get whatever you'd like tonight, Gert. I'm buying."

Her brown eyes snapped up to mine. "No, that's fine, Mr. O—Lauchlan," she corrected. "I'm just—"

"I insist." I interrupted with a warm smile, making sure she knew I wasn't pulling one over her. Well—not that way. "I dragged you out with me tonight, and if I can't get you laid, at least I'll know I got you fed, ay?"

Her little titter melted me a smidge, and I hoped, despite myself, I could get her both tonight.

The server took our order, and I scanned the crowd, determined to do just that. I'd gleaned enough from Gertie tonight, and this wasn't a quick job. I could wait before I started asking the *real* questions.

It wasn't helpful the pair of us looked like a couple having a romantic meal, and I wasn't looking to throw out the impression we were looking for another bedmate.

I was always up for a threesome, but not with Gertie.

Gertie reminded me too much of ... her. The innocence in her smile, the crinkle of her brow at my teasing. The reminder caused a little tug on the hole where my heart used to be. In this light, and a bottle of scotch, I'd mistake her for my little sister.

My gaze caught on a familiar beautiful blonde, seated with a similarly aged brown-haired man in a booth beyond the table area. They looked comfortable, even casual, in their body language, and relaxed, as if this were a routine evening.

He wasn't a lover—they sat too far apart for that—but they had a relationship of some kind. I made a mental note to look into who Hillary Lane was spending her time with after hours at an over-priced taco stand.

Our little table talk at the event the other night made it clear I wasn't the only man Hillary was sleeping with.

I was still doing my research, little by little. Both of my pet projects were working side by side, and I wasn't in a hurry to complete either until all the pieces were properly in place.

The Six never guaranteed a set timeline for their clients —just a time window in which the work would be done. The client paid up front. If the job wasn't completed, they got a percentage of their money back. I'd never heard of such a thing, but I'm sure it happened, just as sure as the sorry sucker they would hire to fulfill a contract never lived to see another one.

I'd need to set another date too. Getting railed in her apartment had its perks, but it was time to go deeper into the world of my beautiful Blondie.

I turned my attention back to Gertie, who'd been chattering away while I was reading the room. I hadn't found any single contenders for a shag mate, so dinner would have to do.

We stuck to comfortable small talk for the rest of dinner, while we ate admittedly delicious food. I came to realize I genuinely liked Gertie's company. Conning was an emotionally isolated life, and it was rare to have any moments of casual chat for the sake of it. I was glad that her part in my plan was relatively innocent. I'd just make sure she didn't get any blowback on account of my ... friendship.

Hillary caught my eye when she sidled out of the booth, abandoning her guest, and made her way down the crammed lane of tables toward me. In a gold silk blouse and copper skirt, she looked radiant as ever.

Her confident strut through the restaurant reminded me once again who I was dealing with. A woman of poise and power, and so much damned sex appeal my cock hurt every time I was around her. This job was significantly better than the time I'd had to seduce a Russian baron whose breath had smelled of turnips and his sack even worse.

"Lucky," she cooed when she got to our table, appraising me with that carefully neutral cadence of hers. "How good to see you."

I stood and brought her in for a kiss on each cheek. "Good to see you, Blondie." I caught a brief sultry smile before her attention turned to my demure friend.

"I'm Hillary Lane." She stuck out her hand for a perfunctory shake, but her smile to Gertie was much warmer than the one I'd gotten. "It's lovely to meet you."

Gertie's eyes widened like she was seeing a mythical sea creature, stunned and somewhat awed. "Yes!" she exclaimed, finally closing her gob to shake Hillary's hand in return. "Of course, I know who you are. Hello—hi. Hi!"

Apparently, meeting me was a hell of a lot less impressive than the likes of billionaire blondies. Perhaps Gertie was attracted to Hillary as much as I was.

"And you are ..." Hillary stared expectantly; Gertie turned a deep rose.

"Gertrude Chicowsky." She smoothed her hands nervously down the front of her jumper. "But please—call me Gertie."

"It's great to meet you, Gertie. I'm glad you're keeping our overseas friend here company."

Hillary's eyes crinkled in barely masked enjoyment, and her gaze snagged on mine for a brief second before turning back to Gertie. "How do you two know each other?"

I shot my hand out under the table to squeeze Gertie's knee in warning, but the gesture was lost in her star-crossed sputter.

"We work together," Gertie blurted quickly, as if she couldn't get the words out fast enough. "Well—we—ah—both work for Mr. Alvarez, but I'm just the assistant. Lauchlan is the tech guy."

Hillary's expression held brief surprise, but then turned indecipherable as she looked me over. I prided myself on being able to read others' secrets like the open book their bodies were, but Hillary was a master at shutting me out.

I preferred to be the one who told my own story, but it was bound to get out eventually. My cover did match the one I'd already told her, even if I'd been intentionally vague.

"See?" A smirk danced along my lips at Blondie's attention. "I'm the tech guy."

"That you are." Hillary scrutinized me for a moment too long before she lit up into a sunny smile, turning all her warmth to Gertie's cherubic face. "It was so nice to meet you, Gertie. Order a bottle of wine on his dollar, okay? Trust me, he's good for it."

With a wave and a laugh, she sauntered away on catwalk heels, leaving me and Gertie to check out a fantastic backside view as the server grabbed her coat.

"You're friends with Hillary Lane?" Gertie hissed once Hillary was out of earshot. "Lauchlan, that's huge!"

Her eyes were shiny with giddy excitement. I was man enough to admit my heart kicked up a notch or two when Hillary was around too. Her wee form had so much *presence*, a Queen to be worshipped on a throne.

And that Queen had come to *me* tonight.

The long con required many steps, and I was slowly moving through each one. A bottle of wine with a sweet Midwest girl was the perfect nightcap to a craic week.

"I'm friends with everybody, Gert." I picked up the wine menu next to our plates and browsed through the American offerings. "You included. What do you say we get some wine and dessert?"

CHAPTER 19

Hillary

Marty: Deal's done. On your desk for the morning.

I shot off a text in response, relieved to have this particular company off my hands. Marty was a gem, working late into the evening once again to help lighten my load. I loved the man.

I stared out the window as Josephine drove down the winding road that led to the base of the mountain. The rich landscape of color, the gold, crimson, and copper of autumn dotting the tops of the trees was the perfect tapestry to calm my roiling mind, even if just for a moment.

We were well outside the clustered city boundary, heading toward the farming fields in the river valley below.

When Lauchlan suggested skydiving as a 'real' date, I had swiftly turned him down and suggested a hot-air balloon ride instead. I liked to play my well-calculated games as much as the next mercenary-trained billionaire, but I was not jumping out of a plane with a man who was after … something.

Naturally, I assumed he was after money; it was usually what everyone wanted from me, after all. I had been pruned and prodded from the time I was born to be a cash cow; for Daddy, for Stanley, Logan … and those were just the blatantly obvious agreements.

I'd fended off many men and women when I came into my grandmother's inheritance. Luckily, being born a Lane and owning several successful businesses already had given me a healthy dose of detachment and suspicion. Opportunistic assholes came and went, bowing out or shoved out before they could make any headway into my head or my heart.

Once I'd built my empire, trusting people no longer mattered. Everyone I did business with was thoroughly vetted. I had very few people in my personal circle, and they were all I needed. Anyone else was just a fun distraction.

Now I knew Lauchlan was working for Alvarez, I wasn't sure what his end goal was, but I was determined to find out.

Neither Alejandro nor Marco knew anything about my personal mission—that I *was* sure of. Other than picking off individual predators, I hadn't even made a dent in the trafficking situation, and the pressing weight of that failure on my chest grew heavier with each new day.

Blackbird had hacked into the HR records and sent them to me this morning; Lauchlan had only worked for the company for a month, just a few weeks after our meeting at Quintessence.

Coincidences, again. Lauchlan was steeped in too many to believe there wasn't a much bigger plan at play.

Josephine drove us out to the grassy field just as the sun dipped toward the horizon, large and orange. I mulled over the situation.

Hot-air balloon rides relied on wind currents, and sunrise or sunset were the best times to float on the breeze. I'd opted for sunset; as much as I believed in '*carpe diem*,' I wasn't interested in spending the first minutes of my morning with a con artist in a farmer's field.

That, and, with my growing nightmares, I'd slept in three times this week. My haunted past roamed my subconscious, pacing deep grooves in the fabric of my mind. I was desperate for a session with Sammy instead of this farce of a date, but curiosity was getting the better of me.

If worse came to worse, Lauchlan could be a stress reliever as a human dildo tonight. There were worse things.

Joey turned onto the short country lane leading to the clearing where Lauchlan was scheduled to meet us. Despite all of my adventures, I'd never taken a hot-air balloon ride before. Logan hated heights, and regardless, it wasn't the kind of couple's activity he and I had ever engaged in.

I could have suggested dinner, but I didn't have the energy to have a long, drawn out conversation with someone who evidently knew how to lie for a living. A person was more truthful when they weren't in a familiar environment. So, Lauchlan and I could dance around 'Two Truths and a Lie' all evening, three thousand feet in the air over a bottle of champagne and strawberries.

It would look and feel like the real thing, and maybe I'd be a few truths closer to figuring him out.

I spotted his candy-colored muscle car long before we came close to it, the unnatural blue a stark contrast to the brilliant orange skyline. As he climbed out of the low driver side door, I took the moment to appreciate the raw sex appeal of Lauchlan O'Donnell before he could see the attraction all over my face.

His outfit reminded me of the first night we'd met. Tight dark denim jeans molded over thick thighs and a full ass—the ass I'd gotten *quite* acquainted with—with dark brown boots. A burgundy sweater peeked out beneath the rugged brown leather jacket that gave him naughty bad-boy energy for days. Aviators covered his mischievous eyes with the setting sun, but the curl of his knowing smirk and messy windswept hair did nothing to hide his 'fuck it' air.

Lucky was a hot piece of ass, and I planned to fuck it a few more times before I sacrificed that sexy body on the altar of my revenge.

I pulled myself together as Joey came to a stop. Then I slid out the rear passenger door to greet my tasty little thief.

"It's great to see you, Blondie."

His solid arms pulled me into a hug before I could get out a word. The unique scent of him—cedar and cherry cola—swallowed me in a cloud of Lucky. For one tiny second, I allowed myself to melt in it.

Even I wasn't immune to the pull of powerful arms and crushing body heat when treading through a lake of problems and crisis. My heart and head didn't need to get involved; I could lean into biology without compromising one second of my greater crusade.

"You too." I pulled out of his hold to flash him a quick smile and tried to step back altogether, but he snared my hand and clamped it in his.

I froze in place, my fingers going limp in his warm grip. Blissful dominating sex was one thing—holding hands like we were some sort of domesticated couple was not the picture perfect postcard I had been going for—even the pretend kind in an empty field in the middle of nowhere.

Still, a ploy's a ploy. I'd done much more for much less potential payback. So I unfroze and squeezed his fingers gently, then I led him toward the corner of the clearing where our balloon ride waited.

"Is she our chaperone this evening?" Lauchlan removed his sunglasses and dipped his head toward Joey still seated stoically in the driver's seat of my Land Rover. "If you wanted an escort tonight, love, I could have just invited a friend."

Joey's gaze tracked us as we walked further out into the field, but she made no move to get out of the car.

"Where I go, Joey goes." I shrugged my shoulders dismissively. "Workplace hazard. She'll wait down here, though."

His stare lingered on my driver/bodyguard for a second longer than casual interest suggested. I stole back his attention.

"Besides, if you're suggesting a threesome, Lucky boy, I'm the one inviting the guest." I licked my lips; his heated gaze followed the trail of the tip of my tongue. "Or do you forget who your master is?"

The sizzling interest in those sea-glass eyes melted into wicked delight. He stopped us in our tracks in the middle of the tall grass and spun me around to face his smirking pout head on.

"Oh, ho! You think because I let you rail me up the arse, you're my Dom now, do ya?" A devious little grin matched the sin in his stare. "Blondie, I believe in equal opportunity. I like to give orders too."

I'll bet.

I snorted, unable to entertain that thought for a second. "Sorry, Lucky." I shook my head with my own sultry smile, sweeping my gaze over the spatter of dark freckles along his cheekbones and the rust-colored stubble along his jaw. "I'm the boss. I'm *always* the boss."

For everyone except one broody Viking and another brutish businessman.

Lauchlan's eyes shifted to the color of stormy seas as he stepped closer. My nose temporarily buried in the folds of the cedar-scented wool atop his hard chest.

"I don't believe *that* for a second, love." His calloused thumb stroked along my jaw and tilted up my head. "Beautiful brats just love a good spanking every now and again to keep that fiery blood in check, ay?"

Okay—I could maybe get on board with that plan.

He kept his grip on my chin and skimmed the other hand up my thigh to possessively cup my hip.

"They do," I said, slightly dipping my head to brush his thumb over the soft flesh of my lip. I parted them slowly, letting the thick digit slip into my mouth and cradling it with my tongue before I sucked hard on the salty skin.

I popped it out with an exaggerated flourish, but the effect was instant. "And I'm the one who spanks them."

A creeping rosy flush colored the pale skin of Lucky's neck, and the blown pupils and granite-hard rod between us told me all I needed to know.

For one fraction of a moment, I let the dark heat of his stare spread warmth through my insides and pull me out of our little gauntlet. For one blissful second, we were just two people in a field about to share the whimsical adventure of childhood dreams.

But I didn't do adventures. I punished pedophiles; maimed and tortured the demons walking as humans. I built cities and organized kingdoms. I wasn't an innocent standing in tall grass at sunset about to share a sweet date with her lover. And neither was Lucky.

We were playing a dangerous game. Each move needed a jarring reminder this dance floor we dallied on was merely a dirty carpet.

I slipped out of his hold before the lust could dissolve my façade of a fact-finding mission into a rudimentary rut.

Pulling his body along with mine, I upped my pace until we stood within the balloon's eight-story shadow. Its rippling kaleidoscope of patterns and colors loomed over us like a joyful mirage.

"We need to leave in three, Ms. Lane!" The young pilot with braided blond hair shouted over the roar of the burner as the balloon was inflating. "We don't want to miss the sunset off Pillar's Peak."

Instead of straining my voice, I nodded my understanding. Lauchlan nestled behind me and we watched the pilot conduct a few more safety checks. His hold to his body probably looked casual, but the weight of his forearms across my chest felt intentional.

"I've always wanted to do this," he whisper-yelled into my ear above the din of the pitchy exhaust. "I'm geeking out, Blondie!"

Agreed. A hot-air balloon was the simplest of science, but it held an allure far more magical than the invention of a modern airplane. I couldn't keep the girlish grin off my face as we stepped onto the platform and lifted off into the sky.

Aside from the aggressive whoosh of the propane flames burning up into the balloon, the ride was exceptionally quiet. Our pilot was silent as she conducted several safety checks and then gave us room to relax—as much room as you could give someone in a 12-by-12 suspended square.

Side by side, we leaned against the perimeter railing as the balloon hovered over the farmland gradually growing distant. Neither of us moved to speak. The feeling of complete weightlessness, like we were birds gliding through the mountain pass, was one of the most peaceful moments I could ever remember.

The chaos in my vengeful veins idled as I drank in every drop of tranquility, forgetting my original intentions for this set-up.

Eventually, Lauchlan broke the silence with a handful of softly uttered words.

"Da would have loved this." His tone was mournful; melancholy. If Lauchlan was using this story as his 'in' for pity points, he was an Oscar-winning actor.

"Oh?" Thanks to Blackbird's sleuthing, I knew his father had died because of a heart attack. I let the question hang in the air—quite literally, wanting him to share the story instead. Needing him to spill his secrets.

"He died. Last year."

The simple explanation made me turn to catch his expression. The sun was just kissing the edge of the horizon behind him. I wasn't prepared for the glossy sheen in his eyes. Was that ... tears? Or just high altitude?

Despite needing distance, I felt compelled to offer comfort. I placed my hand over the icy ridges of his knuckles still gripping the railing, and gently squeezed in reassurance.

"I'm sorry."

"S'alright." Lauchlan's sad smile was laced with something bitter, but I couldn't place it. "He was a good man. Never thought I'd lose him without warning, you know? Still bites."

The child-like mischief Lucky wore as a shield was temporarily down, exposing the points of raw edges beneath. Whatever sport he was playing with me, these emotions were real.

Is this how he played people? Showing vulnerability to get vulnerability? As much as I wanted there to be maliciousness behind his admission, my heart couldn't hide its subtle pang. I knew how the loss of a parent felt to my core.

"My mother died in childbirth." This was a topic I didn't speak about, not even to Winter, but if it would get Lauchlan to open up, bring me closer to figuring him out, and fulfill my retribution, I could let him in on a secret of my own. "I never knew her, and Daddy never spoke about her. I think she would have liked this too."

The admission formed a tight ball of choking emotion at the base of my throat. I swallowed so hard to force it down my mouth was drier than if I had eaten sand.

I'd done my research, of course. Helen Lane had been a stunning ball of energy, a socialite involved in every cause known to man, and loved by all. How she'd ended up with my father was the ultimate puzzle, but somehow, according to every news piece and commentary about her, the opportunistic, egotistical jackal managed to snag himself a good one.

I didn't think about her most days. I didn't want or need the reminder that I'd been robbed of such a formidable woman; that my childhood could have been filled with such light and life, instead of the warped, twisted path my father had led me down.

A strong bicep wrapped around my shoulder, and Lauchlan pulled me tight to the crook of his chest. I huddled within the heat of his body, locking down my emotions before they could reveal any more truths. Who knew a hot-air balloon ride would unlock the vault of *those* memories?

Leaning into Lucky's refuge was not a wise choice, but I didn't care. Vulnerability for vulnerability. Truth for a truth. And I was a liar if I said it wasn't working.

My breathing leveled out—cool pulls of untainted air calmed my nervous system, while the warm pulse of his heart against my cheek did the same. The sun dropped completely below the skyline and the chalky blue of twilight blanketed us as we drifted down to our landing point.

We walked off the platform without a word to each other, greeting the driver who would take us back to our cars, six miles away.

Before I could climb in the passenger seat, Lucky breached my trance.

"I can't believe you call him 'Daddy.' That's weird shyte out of a woman's mouth, unless he's fuckin' ya while you're doin' it."

The moment abruptly broken, I couldn't have been more grateful for the reminder.

A game. This was all a game.

I wouldn't forget it again.

CHAPTER 20

Kellan

Considering I had only visited Sheldonville twice in the past year, twice in the last few weeks was considerable overkill.

Antonio's word was still the law we followed. I had messaged my sociopathic brothers with the directive, and we were meeting at Bourbon & Blues to talk strategy.

I already knew their strategy. Mical would want to kill first, talk later. Jonah was more calculating, but he wouldn't care if we got the information we needed, just that we maximized the enemy's suffering in every way possible.

Antonio's little sycophants.

Of all the killers in our family, I had the lowest body count, despite the underground initiation I had undergone at fifteen, and the rigorous training regime at the Bureau.

Blood and guts didn't turn my stomach or pain my heart, but it did nothing to satisfy my inner demons. Only the complete control of a willing body could offer me that.

I lumbered up the small staircase into the large, paneled office, ready to get this conversation over with. My next task wouldn't be any easier.

Mical's frenzied energy took up an entire half of the room; his broad form bounced on the balls of his feet as he tossed a red stress ball in the air. His shark-like teeth gleamed at me when I walked through the door. He looked to be salivating at the thought of a turf war.

Jonah lazily smoked a joint on the other side of the office, languidly sprawled in a leather wingback. His glazed eyes stared through me when I nodded to him in greeting, as if the entire possibility of bloodshed bored him.

A third figure, a woman, took up the entire middle seat of the matching leather couch. Dressed head to toe in form-fitting black, her feet were firmly planted, as if ready for battle at any moment. I scrutinized her familiar silhouette with a bark to my brothers.

Carmen Williams; *The Devil.* She had lost none of her beauty since the last time I'd seen her, which was at least three years ago. Wavy, jet-black hair fell down her back, matching the bitter chocolate color of her eyes. She fit the runway model profile of Columbian heritage, with wider hips and thick legs – legs used to take down the harshest of men.

"I wasn't aware you had company."

The woman cracked a dangerous smile, full of dark promise and pain.

"Hello, Kellan." The woman's voice was completely void of the Spanish accent that I knew her to have. "It's lovely to see you too."

She had been attractive to me once. I had a relentless affinity for small blondes with big mouths these days. Carmen shifted her weight on the couch and slid to the other end. I sat down on the opposite side, assessing her.

"Where have you been hiding?"

Her smile melted into a condescending smirk. "On a job. I don't just work for these boneheads."

I frowned at her casual dismissal of my brothers. Apparently, a lot had changed between them in the years I had been out of their loop.

"You mean our father. These boneheads"—I nodded to the two men now watching our exchange with interest —"are soldiers, not commanders."

Mical's sneer could have seared through the skin of a lesser man. "I do not need to command armies to prove I have a big cock, brother."

"If you had the biggest cock, you wouldn't need me, no?" Carmen shot back before I could get the chance to reply. My brother's sneer folded into a murderous scowl.

"Chupamela, cono."

A knife whipped out from some hidden place on Carmen's body and speared the ball in Mical's outstretched hand.

"The next time will *be* your cock," she hissed, her threat a self-assured promise.

Jonah's eyes lit up with interest for the first time since I had walked in, and Mical slumped in the adjacent wingback, sulking.

Idiotas, the pair of them.

Ignoring our guest, I turned my attention to the imbeciles of the hour.

"Rally your men. Have everyone on high alert. We don't need this to be a bloody battle, but we need to get this nipped in the bud quickly."

Mical's toddler tantrum transformed into a giddy schoolgirl.

"Bloodshed is not an issue."

"Yes, I know, Mical, you're a big, bad killing machine," I gritted out impatiently. "It's been a slow progression, but with the Rodriguezes shifting alliances, we need to be ready for anything."

I turned to Jonah, my slightly less chaotic brother. "I'm doing my best to keep the Bureau out of this, or else the Cartel will have the Feds on its ass too. We've been able to operate this long without consequences *because* we keep things under control. You know what Antonio will do if we don't."

The threat of our father taking our lives was far more terrifying than law enforcement trying to shut us down. Rampant bribery and several well-placed alliances all over this side of the country made us immune to most punishments, but to die by our father's hands was to die by immeasurably painful torture.

Finally, I had my brothers' undivided attention. We spent the better part of the next two hours reviewing personnel, business arrangements, and dividing territories across the state between our most trusted men.

Carmen's role wasn't clear in the discussion, but Mical informed me she was now working directly for Antonio, and had been invited to this meeting. This situation didn't call for a trained hit woman, but what Antonio wanted, Antonio got.

I was exhausted by the time our chat came to a close, and eager to get away from the gruesome twosome and out of this town. I couldn't have been more grateful for the interrupting phone call.

Abruptly, I stood from the couch and nodded a goodbye as I scanned the number.

"I have to take this."

I stepped out of the office and walked down the narrow staircase toward the side staff entrance.

"Hello?"

"Mr. Carlos."

The male voice on the other end was perfunctorily polite, with the hint of an accent. German, maybe.

"Yes?"

"Thank you very much for your interest in The Six. We've reviewed your contract, but I'm afraid there is a complication with your ... target."

When filling out the request, I'd chosen Hillary as my mark. She was high profile, one of the richest people I could name, and someone I could monitor while The Six were conducting their business. I needed an easy win before this turf war amped up and the FBI caught wind of it.

An issue with the target was not something I'd predicted.

I attempted to keep the irritation out of my response. "What do you mean?"

"At the risk of indiscretion, I'm afraid that target is already ... taken."

My hackles rose at the thought of some other fuck trying to take down Hillary Lane. I made no attempt to keep the ire out of my voice this time.

"What do you mean, 'taken'?"

Brief silence.

"We already have a contract for this person, and we don't take on the same assignment twice, as I'm sure you can understand."

Rising heat took hold of my muscles and my spine stiffened to steel.

"You're telling me that someone else has already selected Hillary Lane as their target?"

"I'm not at liberty to say, sir."

"Well, cancel it." I allowed the threatening tone to fully color my voice—the command I only used to strike fear into the hearts of demons. "I'll pay double the fee. Today."

Finally, a note of fear. "I'm sorry, sir. I—uh—we cannot do that. We take our commitments gravely seriously. I hope you will consider our services in the future."

The line went dead before I could growl out a response.

Who the *fuck* had hired someone to con Hillary?

My plan to put this case in the bag, so I could move on with my more important worries went officially on the back burner as my protective instincts kicked in.

Hillary had refused to let me in; every time I tried to sneak under her defenses to offer a sliver of security, she had pushed me even further away. It was all I could offer her in this fucked up scenario that was my life, and she had stomped all over it with stiletto heels.

The only way in was to give her the help she's asked for; hand her a list to carry out her own twisted vendetta. I could keep an eye on her and work the case at the same time.

It was the lesser, only slightly lesser, of two evils, and yet ...

Fuck.

A harsh breath escaped my lips as I pushed open the wide glass entrance doors. The crisp fall air did nothing to calm the dull thrum of my heart.

My plate was growing heavier with each passing day, and soon the ceramic was going to break. Before it shattered into powdered shards, I needed to keep my brothers in check, manage a turf war, and stave off my father from handing me a despicable empire of sexual slavery.

And kill my lover's lover.
Spectacular.

Four hours of tossing and turning in the makeshift bungalow I called my temporary home was enough to make me want to hurl a television through a window.

I could usually bury the guilt, compartmentalize the atrocities I'd seen and delivered to function throughout the day, but tonight, I couldn't.

Killing men who'd earned their dark souls didn't bother me. Watching the light leave their eyes and the blood seep from their skin was cathartic; one less piece of filth dirtying my shoes.

Aaron was no innocent man—as much as I could be called innocent, and my soul was likely the blackest of them all—but he didn't deserve to die for his parents' crimes.

After another hour of wide-eyed staring at the ceiling, I grabbed my phone from the nightstand, armed with a cocksure plan but steadfast in my decision, consequences be damned.

Kellan: *Antonio doesn't agree to your terms.*

Three minutes later.

Aaron: *Am I to die?*

Yes. But not at my will.

Kellan: *I'll give you a way out.*

Aaron: *Yes?*

Kellan: *Your building. Tuesday night. A fair fight.*

Aaron: *If I win?*

Kellan: *You go free.*

Kellan: *If you lose, you lose your life.*

Aaron: *Agreed.*

Aaron: *I will be there for 10:00 pm. I will be alone.*

The terms were set; the deal was done.

Kellan: *As will I.*

CHAPTER 21

Hillary

"Ms. Lane!"

Gabriella popped up from her perch just outside of Aaron's private suite, her deep red curls bobbing in time with her enthusiastic smile.

I liked Gabriella. She was kind and genuine like a soft kitten, but a fierce tiger whenever someone attempted to go against her employer's wishes. She rivaled Marty in efficiency and tact, and if Aaron downsized anytime soon, I'd snap her up faster than any of his business assets.

I returned her beaming smile with a measured one of my own. "He's not expecting me, Gabby, but I'd like to see him, if he has the time."

"We'll make the time." Her bubble-gum pink lips set into a determined line as she buzzed through the intercom.

"Ms. Lane to see you, sir."

After a few minutes of idle chatter about Gabby's family and a shared love of hot yoga, Aaron appeared in the double-glass doorway. A tight smile overshadowed his sunken eyes.

"Come on in."

I followed his firm backside into the office, enjoying the way his tight gray dress pants lifted each muscular cheek. The crisp, tucked-in white dress shirt he wore lightly wrinkled along his back, hiding the landscape of honed shoulders beneath.

While my office was a bright contrast of white and glass, Aaron's workspace was floor-to-ceiling black lacquered wood and plush dark carpeting.

"For comfort," he'd once told me when I'd teased him about the dust mites collecting within its tufted fabric. *"Dust mites are not my enemy."*

Thick blinds covered the wall of windows overlooking Carlisle's cityscape, and only a dim light at his desk shone downwards to a pile of scattered papers.

He turned a knob next to a panel of switches, and the windows within the doorframe turned opaque, giving us complete privacy.

Aaron walked toward his desk, only fully acknowledging my presence once he'd turned around and leaned against its hulking frame.

Dark tendrils of tousled hair hung loosely behind his ears, and there was a sallow tinge to his normally deeply tanned skin.

I cocked my head, assessing him fully. Aaron Rodriguez might still command a runway and a boardroom, but he looked like shit.

"You've been avoiding me."

The crinkles lining his tired eyes did nothing to make him look better.

"I've been preoccupied, *Mi Reina*. Do not take my absence as a dismissal. How are you?"

Folding my arms across the silk fabric of my blouse, I mirrored his stance.

"I don't think we need to talk about me at the moment. Have you looked in a mirror lately?"

"I've been busy." He ran a large palm through his hair, dropping his caramel eyes from mine. "I have no need for mirrors."

In the years I had known him, I had never seen Aaron as a lost little boy. Despite our recent issues, he had always been a faithful friend, self-assured and never lacking confidence while I was still building my own. He was commanding and direct, and much too literal at times.

But never lost.

The distracted faraway stare into a stack of books on the edge of his desk caused a sharp pang in my twisted heart, and I couldn't help reaching for my old friend.

I stepped into his space, and wrapped my arms around his tapered waist, rubbing a soothing hand down the ridge of his spine. When I rested my ear on his warm chest, the pounding rhythm of his heart drummed against my cheekbone a roiling stampede of torment.

He blew out a slow, deep breath onto the top of my head, ruffling my hair.

"Talk to me." I switched into Spanish, softly crooning the words into the delicate fabric of his shirt. "Tell me, Aaron."

He brought his muscular arms up to my torso and locked me into his embrace. We stood in silence for a few delicate moments before the bass resonance of his voice broke through it.

"I have been given an ultimatum that I do not wish to speak about." His arms tensed around me, forcing me deeper into his chest. "Let me hold you, *Mi Reina*. I want to do nothing else."

The soft plea gave me pause. Busting Aaron's balls was almost a side hobby—the revolving door of sexual tension and shifting power was the very essence of who we'd become to each other—but this moment held a somber need I had never heard him utter.

I wouldn't push him, not today. Tomorrow, we could go back to our usual dance.

I dipped my chin in acknowledgment, digging it into his sternum. He moved his hand up, and caressed my jaw with the pad of his thumb, before tipping my head upward to bring his lips to mine.

He tasted of bourbon and sin, and his mouth manipulated mine in a slow, thorough branding of my body. I'd savored the sweetness of Aaron more times than I could ever count, but this kiss held its own—a drugging claiming instead of the prelude to a fast fuck.

His tongue crept in, slowly wringing every drop of moisture from my mouth and depositing it right into my panties. The bulge of his cock grew between our bodies, pressing hard into my lower belly.

The kiss turned hungry. Soft nips along my neck turned into hard bites against my heated skin, and each grab of teeth filled my insides with molten need. I brought my hands up to his scalp, raked my nails through the silky strands of his mussed hair, and gripped him harder when he ripped the buttons off my blouse with a quick snap of his jaws.

He buried his head between my breasts, the straight line of his nose nuzzling into my cleavage in teasing strokes.

"I need to fuck you, *Mi Reina*." His muffled command hung in the air between us, and his attention stilled on my skin. "I need to feel you wrapped so tightly around my cock, my demons will leave me for just one night."

My body responded, arching into his whispered words as he buried his face back into my chest, biting each nipple through the lace of my purple bra. He impatiently ripped away the rest of my blouse, frantically pulling it off my shoulders and throwing it to the other side of the room.

When he stepped back, eyes glazed with lust, and his cock stiff as steel, I was ragged with want.

In one fluid movement, he turned on his heel and locked the door, then he spun back around wearing a familiar look of determination.

"Will you let me fuck you bare? I have abstained from my employees and my testing is negative."

I hated the feeling of condoms only slightly less than I hated strep throat, but I'd stick to my guns if Aaron was still dabbling with Club 7. I wasn't catching crotch rot, at any cost, from a Rodriguez sex business.

Still, I believed him. In the heat of the moment, I did need to feel the silky heat of his cock spurting inside of me too.

I leveled my wanton stare at his fully dressed body and issued a command of my own. "Fuck me, Aaron." I tilted my head in heated consideration. "Or would you like me to fuck you?"

The rabid glint in his eyes couldn't be misconstrued. He paced the three steps until he once again stood directly in front of me. "Strip me, *Mi Reina.*"

I peered up at him through soft eyelashes before darkening my gaze with a sultry smile. "Yes, sir."

I took my time unbuttoning the crumpled dress shirt, sliding it off his molded arms and gliding my fingers across every inch of skin. I unzipped the dress pants and pushed them down thick thighs until they rested on the floor at his feet. I bent to lift each foot and took them out of their cloth encasement. I rubbed my palms up the crisp hair of his legs before stopping at the hem of his silk boxer briefs to gently squeeze his sac.

His eyes closed and he shuddered beneath my touch as I worked him over until the head of his cock peeked out over the elastic band, glistening with a dewy drop of pre-cum.

Aaron got off on being in control, just as I did. But even more, he loved to be pampered.

I suckled his head into my mouth, licking the drop dry before dipping my tongue into his slit and relishing the demonic shiver as he fisted my hair to maintain his composure. The sharp tingle of pain raked across my scalp, but I wouldn't stop until I had him completely writhing at my mercy.

I peeled the fabric down his legs, continuing to lick down the underside of his cock. Though thick thighs trembled, I held them in place and worked him over until he fully submitted.

"Lay down," I ordered. Unclasping my bra, I tossed it behind Aaron's desk. I shucked my skirt and panties lazily as he watched me from his new place on the carpet, his eyes hovering on the swollen hood of my clit.

I spotted the necktie hanging loosely from a hook and sauntered over. Grabbing it, I brushed the smooth fabric tauntingly across my bare stomach. Molten desire widened his pupils and beckoned me to join him on the downy rug.

He'd done as I asked, displaying his powerful naked body, nestled in a soft cushion like an offering to a goddess.

"Good boy," I purred. Bending over his head, I slid the delicate noose around his neck. I tied the other end to the leg of the nearby coffee table, and cinched it just tight enough to press against his bobbing Adam's apple with a tiny bit of wiggle room.

Aaron's rough palms gripped my thighs as I hovered over him, and my wetness dripped onto the angry flesh of his cock. A stilted grunt escaped his greedy lips just before he yanked me down on top of him.

The friction against my clit shot sparks through my lower belly and up my spine. Our version of foreplay had always resulted in a very satisfying burst of orgasms in quick succession; the throbbing feel of his length between us told me this time would be no different.

I thrust my hips and rubbed myself down the column of his shaft without mercy. The pressure on my clit was the perfect amount to soak his skin.

I grabbed the makeshift collar and slipped a finger underneath to tighten it against his throat.

"I will use you, *Caballero.*" It was a nickname I only dared whisper when we were in this position—when I was riding him and holding him captive within the prison of my thighs.

"I will use you until I can't possibly come anymore. Then, you're going to fill me up so deeply with your massive cock, you'll prove me wrong until I scream again."

His head lolled back, his breathing becoming shallow and measured as he bared his body and neck to me to take as mine to own.

Only Aaron could give me this thrill—this submission—even if I knew it was a test of his own limits of control, not because he enjoyed bowing to me. The underlying reason didn't matter. In this moment, I owned him like he was only worth the human feel of a sizeable dick against my core, and it was all I needed.

I rubbed back and forth, teasing my clit against the swollen head of his cock and then back down again. His cock grew slicker and slicker with each pass. At the crest of my orgasm, he stuffed his palm between my teeth and muffled my screams of ecstasy for only his ears to hear.

I tugged at his collar, tightened my hold, and rubbed harder and faster, until I came for a second time. Before my orgasm was complete, he shoved his cock inside me and thrust upward so hard and so deep I could feel it behind my eyelids.

"Fuuuuuuuuuuuck." I sobbed as he pounded harder and harder, driving my orgasm to impossibly higher heights even as I shattered around him. Within seconds, his cum flooded into me, jet after hot, explosive jet, and I milked him to empty.

We lay within the tangled, sweaty, sticky heap far longer than we ever had, cradled within each other's arms.

The sex was frantic, aggressive, rough, and incredible, as always.

But today felt different.

Aaron wasn't a man who followed his whims. He'd cornered me at our ribbon cutting to make a point, but I had been certain never in a million years would he follow through with his promise.

He liked order and planning. He liked predictability.

This? This frenzied fuck? In his office, no less? Without even a shower to clean his body once we were finished? And cuddling?

Something with Aaron was really, really off.

"Talk to me," I whispered into the scruff of his neck. I'd removed the necktie and positioned myself across his body, snuggling into his warmth and seeking answers from this mystery of a man.

He brought his arms around me, holding on tighter than I'd ever felt him do before.

"I will talk to you tomorrow. Tonight, let me hold you, *Mi Reina.*"

We forgot the outside world for another twenty minutes. The dim sounds of office phones and people speaking just feet away from us filled the space between our beating hearts.

When Joey brought me a change of clothes and took me home for the evening, I couldn't stifle the nagging fear Aaron was in trouble.

If we didn't speak tomorrow, I'd be putting Blackbird to good use.

Aaron wasn't mine, but he was *mine*, and I protected my own.

218

CHAPTER 22

Aaron

He who doesn't fear death dies only once.

Ironically, Giovanni Falcone spent his life prosecuting mafia men in Italy, but the famous line maintained its presence in my thoughts as I walked toward my own end.

I wasn't aimless. Years of honing my body into a sculpted weapon would not be wasted as I fought for my life in the ring of my choosing. I did not hold the untamed ego of a man who believed himself to be invincible.

Practicality weighed into the equation, however. I was not a mafia-trained soldier; I was the ruthless son of

Columbian guerillas, nothing more. I was under no illusions I would walk away from this match unscathed.

Holding my naked queen in the confines of my office had done nothing to quell my resignation, but it had given me purpose. I wasn't fighting for the satisfaction of beating a man who'd done nothing to me, or for the honor of parents who'd dishonored me. Lesser men could maintain my empire of companies.

I hadn't recognized my lack of direction until Kellan presented the ultimatum. I had been living for nothing, working toward nothing more than more money; more power. Neither of these things could satisfy the soul or bring joy to my heart. Yet, they had fueled me for the better part of thirty-five years.

I could not escape Antonio Carlos's sentence any more than I could escape the sadistic intentions of the people who held my name, but I could give them the purest force of my abilities before I bared my neck in submission.

Carefully unfolding the tarp on the still unfinished floor, I taped all along the edges as I waited for my opponent to arrive. The plastic would capture the blood spilled so all evidence of my demise could be melted away instead of trapped beneath floorboards awaiting discovery.

I'd left my last will and testament in a time-locked safe in my office, with written instructions to Spencer, my lawyer, should I not return. I did not name Kellan in its confession, but the document would set enough wheels in motion to lead any uncorrupted authority to my parents' dealings, particularly regarding their recent alliance with Alvarez.

It would be far more convenient had I any evidence of participation in the flesh markets they were so eager to get a cut of the profits from. There was nothing notable yet, but the deal had only been struck for a few weeks, and moving human collateral took time.

My stomach soured in disgust. Men and women chose their lives as best they could in their own circumstances. People choosing to use their bodies was akin to choosing to use intellect or skills to make a living. All humanity had that right.

But to remove choice; to force another being into a life of sexual submission—it was reprehensible beyond words.

I had given Spencer a tattered rope; I could only hope Veronica and Vicente would hang themselves with it.

I paced the squeaky floor as I waited for Kellan to arrive, my thoughts rabid wolves and soothing doves, interchangeably flitting between selfish fear and meditative peace.

Finally, the resounding crack of the metal door echoed through the open space. I'd disabled the security system, not interested in welcoming my guest through the threshold myself. I was resigned to this fate, but unwilling to be its inviting host.

I scrutinized the man walking toward me. He moved on surprisingly silent feet given his considerable size. He'd dressed down in simple black athletic pants and a fitted black undershirt, leaving nothing about his strength or lethal nature to the imagination.

In another life, I would find Kellan attractive; his domineering presence was a soothing balm to my inherent need for an equal partner. Tonight, he was simply the figment of a grim reaper; an obstacle to beat to remain on this side of the soil.

His cheerless nod greeted me when we stood six feet apart on my plastic landscape. I was relieved to note he didn't want to be here anymore than I did—we both took no pleasure in harming those who hadn't harmed us.

We were products of circumstances we'd been gifted at birth; men who tiptoed on lace terraces to maintain the delicate balance of our lives.

"How do you want to deliver your punishment?"

"Antonio's punishment." Kellan was quick to correct me and the rich rumble of his voice rolled over me in the cavernous room. "I'll let you make the first punch."

"No." My tone was sharper than I'd intended, but 'giving' me the advantage was not what this reckoning would be. "First opportunity for a punch will be the first punch. I will not be coddled as you try to kill me, Kellan."

He cocked his shaggy mane in consideration and a respect burned in his eyes I had never seen before.

I'd known Kellan for five years, but I knew nothing about him. He had people collecting the take from our brothels. I'd only seen him at a select few parties when he visited our part of the world. Most his work for the Carlos Cartel was in California, or so the rumors suggested. He was of no consequence to my everyday operations, so I hadn't needed to expend effort on his whereabouts.

He'd captured Hillary's eye when she and Logan were going through their divorce, and it was then that he'd captured my attention too. I'd known it was never our fortune to solely have each other, but I had never considered another woman to permanently take her place.

I had never viewed Kellan as competition, but I had paid attention to how he took care of *Mi Reina*; how he brought out the very best and worst of her, depending on the visit. I watched how he couldn't keep himself out of her orbit when we were all in the same room, but he also would never allow her too close.

If I were removed from this room in a body bag, would she turn him away for good for his crime? Would she mourn my loss?

I shuttered away those thoughts—they would not serve me or stave off my fate.

"Alright." Kellan stepped off the tarp to remove a slew of hidden weapons on his body.

My eyebrows shot up as two guns, a knife, and what looked to be a dart were removed from subtle straps across his calves, waist, and ankle.

He stood and held up his large palms up facing toward me. "No weapons." He resumed his place on the tarp.

When he lowered his shoulders into a fighting stance, I mirrored his image, allowing the waves of acceptance to flow freely into the air between us.

His eyes held an apology, but no words of reassurance were spoken. I didn't want false comfort; I needed this to be done, whatever the outcome.

I jutted out my chin and injected steel into my spine.

"May the best fighter win."

CHAPTER 23

Hillary

Something was very wrong in the universe tonight.

My pumps had worn a circular track in the grooves of the wooden plank floor, as I tried to ease the riotous energy working its way into my bones.

I wasn't a spiritual person. I didn't believe in a higher power orchestrating my every move or that we were destined to follow certain paths. The nature versus nurture philosophy was the one I most subscribed to; had I been born into a humble home on the other side of the planet, I would not be who I was today—full stop.

Circumstances and choices, that's what built our mountain of opportunities and molded our destinies.

Yet I couldn't control the adrenaline coursing through my system tonight, as if my subconscious was fighting for its own life against a torrent of invisible forces.

Aaron hadn't called today. He had failed to put my heightened senses at ease after yesterday's tryst in his office, and his absence had taken up space in my thoughts all day.

I'd slept with Aaron many times; countless times; but the connection we'd shared on his office carpet yesterday had been different. It was raw; a level of vulnerability we'd never shared before. An awakening.

He hadn't called me today, just as he didn't stay to have breakfast with me. Aaron always had a reason that was really an excuse, but today's absence held a dark undercurrent.

When I received the text, the simple message with the words '*Te amo, Mi Reina,*' I knew he was in trouble; permanent, irrevocable trouble.

I stormed to the small closet on the other side of my office, grabbed a tracksuit and a pair of sneakers, and headed into the attached washroom to dress.

"Siri, call Blackbird," I barked to my phone on the vanity, and pulled the tight leggings on over my calves.

I rarely called her late at night, only in an emergency; thousands of years of evolved hind-brain biology was telling me this qualified as one.

"What's up, boss?"

I yanked the dark tank over my head.

"Can you track Aaron's phone for me?"

Unlike Kellan, I rarely checked on Aaron. His whereabouts were predictable and monotonous, rarely warranting a second glance. But I still had Blackbird hack into his GPS years ago as a 'just in case.'

I'd debate my status as a control freak later.

"Sure."

Muffled sounds and the clacks of a keyboard filled my speakers in the absence of words. Thank the universe she'd been at home when I called. Someone else might have been out late on a Tuesday night.

"His phone is at that warehouse in the Crocks. Do you want the address?"

"Yes!" I spit out, zipping up my hoodie and pulling on my trainers.

"Sending now. Oh"—I winced as the shuffle of her phone screeched like nails on a chalkboard in the echoing space —"this is interesting. Kellan's signature is there with him."

I froze my frantic ministrations to get my clothes on.

What in the actual fuck?

Kellan and Aaron didn't play in the same sandbox— ever. Their only connection was their involvement with Antonio's—

Shit.

I didn't have the clairvoyance to understand what was going on, but if Kellan was involved in official Cartel business, this was very, very bad.

"Thanks!" I grabbed the phone and hung up without explanation. Grabbing my keys on the hook by my desk, I raced out the door.

No Joey this time. My Jaguar was parked in the garage below in case I needed to get somewhere in a hurry.

This qualified.

I took the concrete stairs in the emergency stairwell two at a time, urgency licking at my heels like a broiling fire. I couldn't explain the fear making my heart pound nearly out of my chest, but it was there, thrumming like a war drum before the final battle.

The night was eerily dark, cloud cover erasing all evidence of a moon and stars above. I barreled through our city streets with no thought for traffic rules; fortunately, this part of Carlisle completely shut down after eight pm, so I had little competition as I changed lanes like I belonged in a street race.

It took far too long to get to my destination. When I pulled into the parking lot, I caught sight of Aaron's black Mercedes—the car he drove when Jacques wasn't around. Another vehicle, a blue Jeep I didn't recognize, was parked alongside it.

I parked on its opposite side and took one brief moment to catch my bearings. I had no idea who might be in there, what they were doing, or how armed they were. It would be stupid for me to run in empty-handed.

I pulled the dainty handgun out of my glove department. I despised guns, but taking a knife to a gunfight was a stupid move, bound to get me killed. I was a skilled fighter, but I wasn't faster than a bullet.

My phone vibrated against my stomach; I hurriedly pulled it out of my pocket in case it was Blackbird with more information, but it was only Lucky.

He had been trying to get hold of me all evening, but I'd ignored him. I left him on read, again. Our game wasn't important tonight–not when the tangible fear of something amiss was slicing through my insides.

With an impatient sense of caution, I slipped out of the vehicle and pressed myself against the wall of the building. I shuffled along to the large metal entrance door. It hung ajar the tiniest sliver, allowing me to peek into the inside.

Two men circled each other like wary prey, blood trickling from their knuckles, grim determination on their faces.

My two men. Aaron took Kellan's punch, and blood sprayed from his face along with an echoing grunt of pain.

I couldn't see anyone else from my vantage point, and I couldn't stand by while these insufferable asshats beat each other to death.

I kicked in the door with a flourish, raised my gun in front of my face, and conducted a quick perimeter check.

We were alone. Neither man turned to look at me, too lost in their caveman dance to notice my presence.

I watched in horror as Aaron got in a hit; Kellan grunted and fell to his knees at the gut punch, but then, he caught Aaron right in the solar plexus, dropping him to the ground. He rolled on top of Aaron's wheezing form, and raised a fist to pound his face.

I couldn't think—couldn't breathe—so I shot instead.

The crack of the bullet rocketed through the empty space like a sonic boom and it wedged into a steel beam on the other side of the room. Two haunted gazes turned to look at me in shock.

"What in the ever-loving *fuck* are you doing here?"

The first to recover his voice, Kellan's icy gaze was furious as he stared at the gun in my hand. An angled gash bled over his right eyelid, leaving a streak of blood down his cheek that clumped into the light hair of his beard. The raw skin of his fists was a stark contrast to his black clothing.

"You should not be here, *Mi Reina*," Aaron said from his battered position on the ground. "We have not settled this dispute yet."

I stared at him in frustrated disbelief before leveling my gun on Kellan's wrathful face. "Excuse me? What the fuck are *you* doing here? Why the *fuck* are you trying to kill each other?"

My voice escalated from delivering a simple question to an incensed shriek. In any other circumstance, I would pride myself on staying calm and kept my emotions beneath the surface, disallowing any vulnerability to show. I'd bury any sign of weakness to maintain my powerful persona.

All of my training and hard-won skill at negotiation had escaped through the crack in the metal door.

Watching the two of them intentionally trying to destroy each other broke something in me. I wasn't leaving here without the two of them intact, or they could put me in a body bag too.

I had no suicidal impulses, so that definitely wouldn't be happening tonight.

"How did you know we were here?" Aaron's ragged voice posed the question, but Kellan answered it.

"She tracks us." His grunt held the severe tone of displeasure. "You have some serious control issues, Killer."

I cocked the gun and gestured for Kellan to move away from Aaron's limp body. "Get away from him. And somebody better fucking tell me what this is about. *Now.*"

Aaron's sigh broke through bloodied, swollen lips.

"Kellan is delivering justice," he said simply, wincing as he rolled his body to the side and pushed himself into a seated position. "My parents have failed Antonio, and I must pay the price."

"Are you fucking serious?"

My stunned expression morphed into a raging glare at the hulking Viking drenched in scrapes and still on his knees.

"What the fuck, Kellan?"

A flicker of remorse rippled through his stare, but then it was gone.

"Just kill me and get it over with, Hillary. That's the easiest way out for me. I follow orders or I'm the one who dies. I gave Aaron a choice, and he chose a fair fight."

I stepped back, stunned at his dispassionate declaration. "You think I'm going to kill you? Not a chance. But I will give you a fair fight."

I dropped the gun, flinching at the finality of the thunk on the plywood floor. I swept my hair up into a ponytail, then shrugged off my sweater and turned to face the two men with a renewed sense of purpose.

"You wanted a fair fight, Viking? I'm tapping in for Aaron. You can fight me."

My blond god blinked rapidly before shaking his head in vehemence. "Not a fucking chance, Hill."

"No." I held up a finger, the finality in my tone brooking no arguments. "One more hit to the head, and he'll be out. Look at him." I swept my arm out like Vanna White at the mound of brutalized flesh that was Aaron Rodriguez. "I'm trained, and you're tired. I can't think of a fairer fight."

"No." Kellan's growl reverberated through me; Aaron's matching protest settled under my skin, but I held my ground.

"If I win, I won't kill you, and the three of us can figure out what our next steps are together." I blew out a breath and stared into the frosted pools of my lover's eyes, imploring him to see the truth.

"If either of you dies, Kellan, I might as well be dead too." I walked toward him, daring to rest my palms on his shoulders as his relentless, angry eyes glared up at me. "I refuse to let either of you go for the shitty decisions of your parents. Fight me."

I couldn't break eye contact, but I reached out my hand blindly for Aaron's, needing his solidarity as I stood for his salvation. He was close to death, and if he refused me now

...

Relief flooded through me when his palm slid against mine, interlocking our fingers and squeezing gently.

"I do not want this for you," Aaron wheezed, "but I can never refuse you, *Mi Reina*. Kellan will not kill you."

"No, I won't," Kellan bit out angrily, his voice lanced with venomous ire. "But if this is how she chooses to stop this, I'll play the game. A fair fight, Killer."

He rose from his knees and held out his hand. I released Aaron and shook Kellan's calloused palm, gripping it fiercely in an attempt to relay everything my mouth couldn't say.

I care for you. I care for him. This isn't the way out. We can be allies; partners; friends.

I would prove it to him. With fists, kicks, and Krav Maga tricks.

"May the best woman win."

CHAPTER 24

Lauchlan

Tuesday nights were feckin' boring.

I'd been pestering my pretty little Blondie all evening to come out to play with me, but she wasn't answering my messages.

She was a busy woman, and I was still working my way into her heart, but I'd thought a time or two since our date in the balloon that the whole connection thing might have gotten a wee too … much.

I was as surprised to get choked up as she was—Da's sense of adventure and the recent loss of him still snuck behind my eyelids every now and again.

Apparently, now and then included riding air currents with a beautiful woman I was trying to cheat. Lovely timing, and all that.

Still, women loved vulnerability. Ol' Brene Brown woulda been proud of that whole touchy-feely moment. Of course, I knew her ma had passed—I'd done my research—but hearing her tell it; well, that made it a bit more real for me too.

I didn't like when marks started looking like people. When they were people, it complicated things. Better to see them only as jobs with a dividend at the end.

Simple. Easy. *Un*complicated.

I was feeling a whole lot of complicatedness tonight, and I wanted my Blondie to peg it out of me again. A good ol' prostate poke would remind me of the mission and give me some more spank bank material to boot.

Win-win.

I was sprawled on Ma's couch while she was out working a job, flipping through American porn channels with disinterest. My mind constantly flit back to the naked Queen rubbing herself all over me. A naked lass rubbing her tits on a 2-D screen was right boring by comparison. I flicked off the TV and grabbed my phone instead.

In Dublin, I had buddies to call on when I was bored out of my tree. We'd grab a pint or play football at the pitch. Here, I only had jobs and Ma. Neither would suit my interests tonight.

After a half hour of twiddling my thumbs playing *Candy Crush*, my restlessness got the better of me. I decided to check on my tasty little treat for shits and giggles more than anything.

Not at all because I was becoming obsessed with her.

I'd slipped a micro tracker on her cellphone when she'd sidled up to me after our dead parents' confessional. Made me feel a bit shyte to be honest, but seizing opportunities was the name of the con game, and I couldn't have asked for a better one.

I had designed the chip myself. A sneaky little speck the size of a dirt smudge, which could only do one thing—broadcast a location.

I opened the app on my phone, and cracked my neck and knuckles in the few seconds it took to load. The flashing hot pink dot—did that on purpose—came into view, moving at the speed of a vehicle down a dodgier part of the industrial core.

What was my Blondie doing down in the Crocks at ten-thirty on a Tuesday?

Curiosity made me giddy, and now I had a mystery to solve with my beautiful billionaire at the center. I clapped my hands in glee before leaping to my feet, grabbed the keys off the counter, and jumped in the elevator down the 10 floors to my car park.

I knew everything there was to know about Hillary that had been recorded on paper, but I still knew so little. What would I find out tonight? Was she a secret dancer? A stripper? Did she have a mafia lover?

I mulled over many theories, each more ridiculous and sexier than the last, as I drove toward her pretty pink little dot now stopped in a warehouse parking lot.

Whatever she was doing, I wouldn't be staying; I was just taking a little peeky-boo at what my mysterious mark spent her time doing on a drab Tuesday.

Unless she was taking part in an underground orgy in one of those done-up abandoned buildings filled with hot, sexually repressed power women. Then I was *definitely* staying.

I was always up for an orgy.

I pulled in next to three cars, none of them recognizable, and parked, grabbing my gun and my switchblade from the center console, just in case.

Never bring a knife to a gunfight; but if it's a knife fight … bring a knife *and* a gun. Da had some wisdom, all right.

I hadn't felt threatened once since settling into Carlisle. The people here were much softer than the powers I was used to in Europe, but Americans were much more subtle about their threats and intents. I didn't feel the need for weapons, but I went nowhere empty-handed.

Muffled grunts and gasps crept out of the door, and the prospect of an actual sex party delighted me, until I caught an aggressive growl with my Blondie's name on the air.

"Hillary. I don't want to kill you!"

Kill her? The fuck was I walking into?

I didn't think—something Ma would say I do often, but she'd be wrong—and swung the door open with my weapon raised.

I was not prepared to see a scrappy blonde woman sweeping the legs out from under muscular Thor. The two of them landed in a heap on a crackly—*was that a tarp?*—floor beneath them.

Hillary didn't slow. Leaping from her position just shy of Kellan's head, she circled him as he rose to his feet just as deftly. The pair of them faced me with rabid faces, blood streaked across their skin in mismatched patterns.

Kellan looked like *Wolverine* himself had clawed him across the cheeks. Aaron, the Rodriguez patsy, sat on the outside of the makeshift fight ring *thing*, his hawkish gaze watching me like his eyeballs were glued to my forehead. The man was a bit of a robot, not even blinking at me before turning his psycho-stare back on Blondie.

Surprised he could see anything through two swollen black eyes.

"The fuck is this?" I asked, maintaining my composure in case they added me to the ring. "Some sort of fucked up fight club for rich kids?"

Kellan reached for something on the floor, and before I could blink, a black handgun was pointed in my direction, the safety unlocked and ready to skewer some Irish blood.

"I don't want to shoot you, Conan, but I'm not willing for Blondie to lose a limb tonight." I kept my gun trained on him, nodding my head toward the door. "Toss it."

Another metallic click of a bullet in a chamber startled me. Hillary held her own pretty little silver gun in her grip, and by the look in her eyes, she knew how to use it.

"Drop the gun, Lucky. You shouldn't be here."

Lord have mercy. If this woman got any sexier, I'd be locking her up in my bedroom til the end of time.

"Jesus, Blondie. I'm trying to rescue you from a fuckin' barbarian, here. Mind telling me why you're all exorcising your demons on each other?"

I'd let her exorcise her demons on me. Her split lip, flushed face, and bruised torso in a sports bra made her look like a warrior straight out of hell. Turns out, I was into that.

The faint whistle of metal zipping through the air was my only warning a blade was coming for me, but I was too late.

"Fuck!" I roared. A tiny but lethal throwing dagger speared my right hand. I dropped the gun and gripped my wrist. My gaze snapped to a now very-alert Aaron who glared metaphorical daggers back at me too.

The three of them started firing off words in rapid Spanish, their attention and weapons no longer trained on me while I bled rivulets all over the unfinished floor. Now that I was impaled, I wasn't a threat or something.

"I don't like your friends, Blondie," I muttered as I tore off the sleeve of my shirt and wrapped it around my wrist as a makeshift tourniquet.

I sat down on the floor, listening to the three of them angrily snap at each other; fully willing to wait them out.

Con men were patient. This certainly wasn't the stickiest situation I'd ever gotten myself into. I was semi-confident, if worse came to worse Hillary wouldn't kill me.

Mostly.

Plus, I couldn't complain it was a boring Tuesday night anymore.

It wasn't until a name—Alvarez—cropped up that I snapped to attention.

"What the fuck do you lot want with Alvarez?"

Their attention turned back to me. The three of them stared at me with suspicious eyes filled with dark intent. I didn't like where this was going.

The bloodied man who looked every bit a real-life Viking stalked over to me and gripped my shoulder with a massive mitt, dragging me forward onto the plastic pooled with little puddles of blood.

More rapid-fire Spanish with aggressive hand gestures. Arguing and counter-arguing. Mostly debating whether or not to off me, if I was reading the room right.

When Kellan cocked his gun at my head again, stress sweat beaded along my hairline.

She wouldn't let him kill me, would she? Not my Blondie?

The thought died a fiery death when her own gun came up to point—I was too fixated on Kellan's weapon, I couldn't tell where it was aimed exactly, but I had my suspicions.

"We will see what he knows."

Aaron's voice broke through their squabble. Had to give the guy credit, he could be as commanding as the other two, even with a smucked up face. He rose from his courtside seat and limped toward me.

Okay, now I was probably in real trouble.

The three stared down at me, all imposing and angry, and I started calculating how I was going to get out of this mess. A bit late, really, but I'd really been convinced I'd made enough inroads with Blondie I wouldn't need to. Hopefully, I could live and learn for the next job.

It didn't look promising.

Snarled Spanish. Insults. Three Alphas with their little Beta cornered. If I could just–

Hillary's English reply broke through the noise.

"Lauchlan," she stated coolly. My full name dripped with false security off her devilish tongue. "It's your *lucky* day. Welcome to Fight Club. If you want to walk out of here alive, here's your initiation."

Fuck.

Nope.

I didn't like that one bit.

Uh, oh. Looks like the Rook is caught! How is Lucky going to get out of this mess?

In the ultimate game of cat and mouse, who will be the victor?

The Rook, The Knight, The King, or the Queen?

Find out in To Curse a Knight, All the Queen's Men, Book 2 – available for pre-order today!

Other books by Cora Flynn

<u>Cascade of Lies (series)</u>
Days of Winter
Nights of Winter
Winter's End